Fly With A Dragon

By Rosemary Laurey

A virgin sacrifice, a not-so ravening dragon and a happy ever after.

Selected as the virgin sacrifice to the ravening dragon, Myfanwy awaits as Arragh, the fiery Dragon of Cader Bala, approaches across the sacred grove.

But Arragh comes not to destroy. Instead he carries Myfanwy off to his domain in the far mountains, and a fate far, far better than death.

Warning, this title contains: unusual and pretty much impossible explicit sex.

Heart of the Raven
By J.C. Wilder

Sold into slavery to an Overseer of the Realm, Dani is determined to win her freedom and make sure her heart is possessed by no man.

For Haaken, time is running out. A family curse already condemns him to the form of the Raven and when he can find the one woman meant for him, only then will he be free.

Too bad for both of them that this woman is determined to belong to no one...

Warning, this title contains: HOT, explicit sex.

Sacrifice

A Samhain Publishing, Ltd. publication.

Samhain Publishing, Ltd.
577 Mulberry Street, Suite 1520
Macon, GA 31201
www.samhainpublishing.com

Sacrifice
Print ISBN: 978-1-59998-298-4
Fly with a Dragon Copyright © 2008 by Rosemary Laurey
Heart of the Raven Copyright © 2008 by J.C. Wilder

Editing by Jessica Bimberg
Cover by Scott Carpenter

Published electronically as Paradox I, ISBN 1-59998-223-4
First Samhain Publishing, Ltd. electronic publication: September 2006
First Samhain Publishing, Ltd. print publication: June 2008

Contents

Fly With a Dragon

Rosemary Laurey

Dedication

For George.

Chapter One

It was too late for prayers or petitions. She was alone. Deserted. The others had fled, abandoning her at the first rumble like distant thunder.

Myfanwy gathered the last shreds of her courage and suppressed the shivers of fear. She couldn't run. Stout ropes bound her to the sacred oak. Shoulders back and her chin up, she waited for the approaching dragon. He would not see her terror. She would die with the courage befitting her father's daughter. But despite all her resolve, her mouth gaped and a soft gasp of surprise escaped her dry throat at her first sight of the ravager.

He stood upright, not crawling like a worm but standing erect and striding toward her like a man. But one look told her he was not a man. The dragon stopped a little more than an arm's length from where she waited, bound tight and terrified.

He was taller than her brothers and broader in the chest than her father and his pale gray skin gleamed in the twilight. He said nothing for several long minutes, just stood not quite close enough to touch her. He let his green eyes gaze from her face to her bare feet and back to meet her eyes, catching them with an intensity that made her shiver against her will.

"So," the dragon's voice was warm, rich, and as intoxicating as a tankard of aged mead, "you are the sacrifice prepared for me."

She held herself as tall as anyone could tied to a tree and replied, "I am Myfanwy, daughter of—"

"Harwed Rees, the village chieftain," he finished for her, his strange wide gray lips curling in a twisted half-smile. "Could they find no other to offer me, that the chief's own daughter stands here? Or did your father think to placate me with his own offspring?"

Myfanwy suppressed a shudder. Willing herself to show no weakness to this terror, she let the rough trunk of the tree support her weakening legs. Not that she could have run if she'd chosen. They'd used the finest ropes the weavers could provide. The tight flax cut into her arms and thighs, chafing her waist through the thin shift that was all they had permitted her to wear. She was helpless, the next best thing to naked, and the scourge of the countryside stood an arm's length away.

The scourge of the countryside smiled, his mouth wide, his eyes almost twinkling. With what? Amusement at her plight? Anticipation of his next meal? The ridges over his eyes rose as his scaly forehead rippled. He cocked his head, waiting for her answer, enjoying her discomfort—or was he? His eyes seemed almost gentle as they met hers. Impossible! This was the worm who'd ravaged their crops and slaughtered the other maidens sacrificed to his ravening.

"You find me unsuitable, sir?"

That truly amused him. His eyes gleamed green as spring grass in sunshine as his wide lips creased into a broad smile. "No, sweet sacrifice, I find you most...suitable...for my purpose." Myfanwy shivered, imagining his purpose. "I just wonder why your father chose to honor me with his only daughter instead of some buxom peasant."

"I think that is partly your fault, sir."

"Mine? How so?" His eyes widened with the surprise in his voice. "I've been blamed for pillage, disaster, and ravage of the countryside but it was your father who chose you and your brothers who lashed you to the sacrificial oak."

"Yes," she conceded, biting her lip as she remembered, half-wondering how he knew. Had he seen her brought out here? "But you let it be known you wanted…" she hesitated, "a virgin."

He shrugged and rippled the great muscles beneath his gray skin. "And why not? The Dragon of Cader Bala takes no human's cast-off."

"Yes…but when the word spread that you insisted on virgin tribute, most of the village maidens took pains to ensure they were no longer suitable for offering."

The destroyer laughed. He threw back his great head with a wild dragon roar that had the birds in the trees deserting their roosts. As his laughter faded, he met her eyes and gave a soft chuckle that sent a warm shiver rippling across her skin. "So, my demands precipitated a great orgy. Though I doubt it was an onerous duty for the chosen swains." The ravager of the countryside stepped closer and Myfanwy caught his scent— sweet wood smoke, like an apple or pear log tossed on the fires in her father's hall. His breath came warm and sweet on her face. "And how did you escape this great fuck of defiance? Are the men of your father's demesne blind, or just plain stupid?"

"My father and brothers were watchful. They wanted me kept pure for my husband."

The dragon nodded. "So, some worthy warrior has been robbed of a bride." The idea amused him. She heard it in the

13

lightness of his voice and couldn't miss the almost blue sparkle deep in his darkening green eyes. "And now, you offer me what he will never enjoy."

A warm shiver raced from her face to between her legs. She looked up at the dragon, her face burning and her body warm with a heat she only half-understood, and that half-disturbed her. Greatly. Praise the Goddess the dragon had no cock—she was safe from rape. She had prepared herself to die but... Myfanwy took a deep breath, to steady her nerves as much as her racing heart. "Sir, what do you wish of me?"

"Everything, Myfanwy," the dragon replied. As he spoke, he reached out his right arm, his long gray fingers bare inches from her face. The back of his hand was crosshatched with dark lines like the veins on a leaf or the fine detail of a seashell. He flexed his fingers and the muscles showed the strength in even his littlest finger. As she watched, great claws extended, just as a cat might prepare to scratch against furniture. But this was no house cat to be gathered up and held on her lap. This was the Dragon of Cader Bala and she was his victim. She could not stop trembling.

"Be still, I will not hurt you." She had no reason to trust his word, but looking into his deep green eyes, believe him she did.

Even so, her heartbeat sped fast as a frightened bird's as one fine-pointed claw drew a line down her shift from her neck to her waist. She felt warmth and smelled burning linen. She glanced down in horror. He'd burned her bodice apart!

"Hush," he whispered as she opened her mouth to protest, cry, or perhaps whimper. His strong hands brushed the singed halves of her shift away from her breasts. His touch was strangely gentle, calming her fears as the pads of his fingers brushed her chest. Was it his hands or the chill breeze of the glade that turned her skin into chicken flesh? Her exposed breasts lay open to the air and the dragon's gaze. Her nipples hardened like the young acorns on the tree overhead, and the smile on his gray lips sent a fire coursing through her veins.

"Your father flatters me with his gift," the dragon said as he cupped her shoulder with a warm hand. "And your generosity, lady, honors me. While some less virtuous maid goes to your intended groom, you offer yourself to the Dragon's embrace."

"Hardly that! I didn't exactly tie myself to this tree!" Her fear made her say more than was wise. Would he blast her for her impudence?

Seemingly not. At least not yet. "No, your caring and vigilant brothers did that at your father's command."

That much was true. They'd roped her securely and then run as if the dragon were already at their heels. "What do you want?" Why ask? She'd seen the charred remains of his other victims, her cousin Bron last spring, Mary the weaver's club-footed daughter the year before.

"I want you, Myfanwy, daughter of Harwed Rees. Will you come with me?"

"I have a choice?" She'd have laughed if her heart wasn't tight with fear.

He considered it a valid question. "Lady, there are always choices. I chose this valley to hunt, your father chose you as my delight. And I ask you, will you come with me?" He stepped back a stride. She missed his warmth—his closeness had protected her from the cool air. She shivered as he watched her with unblinking green eyes. Waiting. His face blank as a mask. What would he do if she refused?

The possibility died even before her mind put words to it. If she could save her family and clan from his pestilence, so be it. "I will come with you, sir, on condition you keep your word to leave my valley unmolested for...five years." She all but gasped

15

at her temerity. She was haggling with the scourge of the valley as if he were a wandering peddler.

He was amused, not angered. "You would bargain with me, lady?" An eyebrow ridge rose as he spoke.

"What have I to lose? My fate is sealed but I would save others if I can."

He inclined his head, like a warrior acknowledging a commission. "You have the word of the Dragon of Cader Bala. Come with me freely and obey me completely and your people will be safe."

Inexplicably, she believed him. Of course he'd said nothing about her safety. May the Goddess give her courage to face her end! The dragon didn't move. Just stood, watching her, his mouth twitching at one corner as if pleased with what he saw. She shivered, forcing herself to breathe slowly. She'd face death with the best dignity she could muster. A gray tongue slipped from his almost-closed mouth. Slowly he licked his lips. A cold shudder took her, retching its way from her chest to her feet, pulling her brain with it, and tearing at her resolve.

"Sir..." she began, her voice shaking and weak.

"My name is Arragh."

So, she was to know the name of her slayer. "Arragh," she paused, "how long before—"

"I consume you, sweet Myfanwy, and you and I become one?" Hearing it so blandly from his lips sent a cold shiver down her spine. "Not long, lady, but not here. This is not the place."

Her mouth dropped open at that. "But this is the appointed place." The others had all perished on the edge of the sacred grove.

"Chosen by your people, lady, not by me." He took a half-step closer. "You consented to come with me. I choose where we go."

So, he would take her away to slaughter her. How would he kill her? Throttle her? Rip her apart with those strong, skin-clad arms and sharp claws? Burn her alive as the others had perished? Despite her resolve, her courage faltered. The evening air on her naked breasts echoed the chill in her soul. Was this to be the end of all her hopes and dreams? Death in the hands of a dragon? If so, she begged the Goddess to help her bear it with courage.

Arragh took another step. He was so close now, if she were unbound, she could have reached out and traced the lines of scale in his gray skin, run her fingers along the green ridges on his shoulders. If she were unbound, she could have fled. But her hands were lashed together against the rough bark of the sacred oak and her legs were tied with twisted rope and even if free, how could she flee and put her life above her people's safety?

She had put her trust in the word of a worm and would die to save others from her dreadful fate.

Arragh's mouth twitched at one corner as he leaned forward, lips slightly parted, and brushed the fabric of her shift right off her shoulders. His touch was gentle, his skin smooth and strangely warm against hers as he drew his fingers across her chest. He said nothing, his eyes intent on her face, as his sheathed, and now blunt, claws traced a wild ribbon of sensation from one shoulder to the other, pausing in the hollow of her neck to rest his splayed hand on the flat above her breasts.

The tree at her back prevented movement, even if she had wished to evade the confident trail of his fingers. He rested his other hand flat on the tree beside her face. She was pinioned, held fast by his presence and his will and the knots of her brothers' making. Her breath came in short, shallow spurts as he lowered his head.

Myfanwy braced herself for the rent of his teeth in her throat, but his warm breath skimmed her bared breast. Before she thought to flinch or cry out, his tongue moistened her shivering flesh and his lips closed over her nipple, like a babe suckling his nurse.

For a slow second, her breathing ceased and her heart skittered, then a wild warmth flooded her consciousness, like a stream in full spate, or a wild forest fire. She gasped but not from fear or pain. A wild weakness took her, and without the oak at her back and the ropes circling her waist, she'd have collapsed on the grassy turf. Arragh lifted his mouth away and the evening air gave a sudden chill to her now-moist nipple, as he moved to take her other breast.

This time she expected the warmth in her bones but not the slow sweet yearning that rose deep in her vitals to pool between her legs. She fought with all her will to restrain the moan that started deep in her throat, but a slow sigh escaped her clenched lips. Her eyes widened at the sound of her own need. Her heart raced as she glanced down at the dragon. His face was hidden against the whiteness of her breast, his head a hard dark shape in the gathering gloom. She longed to take her hands and cup the firm roundness of his skull, to know how his strange, veined skin felt under her fingertips. The touch of his hand and lips and the press of his face on her breasts told her he was neither slimy nor scaly as the bards insisted. Arragh was not the crawling worm of song, nor the destroyer of the legends. Or was he?

She sighed as he lifted his head and fixed her with his deep green eyes. Blue lights glimmered in their depths. He had no eyelashes, no hair that she could see, just two immense eyes in his great face. He was a creature of the far mountains, the bringer of fire and destruction, the destroyer. He held her in his absolute power, touched her with gentleness, and looked at her with kindness.

Nonsense! He was a monster, an animal incapable of kindly thoughts, a creature of devastation who stripped her near-naked with tender hands and caressed her nipples with his warm lips and would very soon consume her with fire, or rip her limbs from her body and...

It took all she had not to whimper her disappointment.

"You will come with me then, Myfanwy? Freely? Willing to follow my direction?"

"Yes." Did he think she would refuse?

His eyes glimmered as he stood upright. Still resting one hand on the tree above her head, he reached out and stroked her cheek with the back of his free hand. His skin was smooth, if a little dry, and his touch sent the same wild sensations coursing through her. Would he consume her soon? Did he enjoy playing with her before the kill? Teasing her like a cat with a helpless bird? She shook at the thought.

"Be still," he said, holding her to the tree.

The bark was rough against her back. His hand held firm on her shoulder. She should be terrified but a strange calm enveloped her. She was no longer afraid. Perhaps she was past fear.

His right arm moved, his index finger raised. With a swift, almost unseen movement, he flashed a narrow thread of fire down her side. Myfanwy gasped, smelled burning rope, and watched her bonds fall away into a smoking heap on the grass. She stepped away from the smoldering rope into Arragh's arms.

"Steady," he whispered in her ear, running his hands over her back and head, as if to calm a frightened animal. "Be still."

The wide fingers that had burned her bonds moments earlier rubbed her wrists and arms, chafing her skin back to life. Satisfied the circulation in her arms had returned, he knelt. His hands now rubbed her ankles, easing the pain from the ropes and sending sweet shivers coursing through her body. Unable to stop herself, now that her arms were free, she rested a hand on his smooth skull.

He paused a second at her touch and she froze, fearing she'd angered him, but he continued the gentle caress of her legs. Emboldened, she rested both hands on his scalp.

His skin was smooth and cool, but warmed under her touch. A ridge of raised skin, hard like the callus of a sword hand, ran from his crown down his back where a man would have a spine. Wide green and gray ridges ran across his shoulders and back, like the veins on the underside of a leaf, or the markings of a dragonfly's wings. Was this why they were so named? She smiled, very unsure of herself...and Arragh.

He had neither attacked nor harmed her. His voice was calm, almost soothing, and his touch as gentle as a nurse's. His head was as smooth and soft as an infant's and...

She gave a gasp as he stood and in one movement pushed the remains of her shift to the ground. She was naked and he...

He took her hand. Easily. As if to steady and balance, not to restrain her. "Step away from it," he said.

She obeyed, nervous with the awareness of her total nudity.

Holding her at arm's length, Arragh surveyed her, like a horseman regarding a new mount. "Leave that behind," he said, glancing at the pile of rags lying at her feet. "It will only hinder you and it burns too easily." Why did that matter? Was he going to kill her after all? "Your hair." As he spoke he ran his fingers down one braid. "That must go."

"Why, sir?" Her much admired copper-colored braids were her vanity and to lose them...

"Human hair burns too easily," he replied and as if to prove his point, with a flick of his fingers, he burned off her braids, pinching the ends between his fingers to extinguish the flame.

Myfanwy gasped as her braids dropped to her feet, the smell of burning hair still hanging in the air. Was this a preliminary to her sacrifice? What would he do to her next?

"Are your legs strong enough to run?" he asked.

Run? So he was going to play with her and chase her like a hunted animal. "I can run if I need, sir. But whom would I need to flee from?" She kept her chin high and prayed her voice didn't falter.

"Whom would we flee from?" Arragh echoed with a slow twist of one corner of his mouth. "From your father's warriors who wait beyond the grove with their fire and staves." She opened her mouth to speak but Arragh shook his head and rested a finger on her lips. "Later, Myfanwy, ask your questions. Time passes and we must leave. When I give the word, run. Do not let go of me and never stop. If you hesitate, you will perish."

Chapter Two

She shivered at the threat. A threat spoken kindly, as if he cared for her to live. His words barely made sense. Her father meant her no harm. There had been tears in his eyes as her brothers took her away.

"Come." Arragh's hand closed over hers, and he drew her close. "Remember your promise, Myfanwy. To obey."

"I gave my word."

"Yes." A trace of a smile curled a corner of his mouth. "You did." He paused, his hand on her shoulder. "Will you also give me a kiss from your lips?" Her throat clenched at his question. Why would he ask this? "I mean you no harm, Myfanwy." Could she believe him? Trust him? He asked for what he could have taken with ease, whether she wished or not. He asked for no more than she'd given her cousin Arden at the last winter revels.

Her mouth was too dry to speak so she looked Arragh in the eye and nodded.

He breathed warmth on her face as his mouth closed over hers. His lips were cold and soft and heated and hard all at once. She gasped at his touch and at once felt his tongue—long, narrow and strong. Certainly, confidently, he circled her mouth, caressing the inside of her cheeks, gliding over her tongue and pulsing gently against her teeth. It felt strange and wonderful and frightening and she dreaded him stopping.

A strange fluidity seeped through her limbs, her legs weakened, her body went heavy, and she leaned against the dragon, molding herself into his hard frame, wrapping her arms around his broad back. His skin was cool and firm and warmed as she pressed against him. His strong arms held her close, his hands wide and smooth on her skin, his fingers playing a tattoo on her bare back, in a gentle mark of possession, a sweet sensation of pleasure. She sighed into his kiss. Lost in the wild feelings charging through her body, Myfanwy half-heard Arragh groan against her mouth as he drew away, still holding her close, his breath coming fast and his heart racing under his firm chest. She ran her hands over his skin as if to learn more of this creature who held and embraced her.

"Sweet one," he said. His lips were wide and swollen, just as hers felt. She smiled up at him and watched his eyes flicker blue. "You would have us both killed as we stand here. Come." He took her hand in his and strode across the glade. "Be ready to run for your life when I give the word."

How could he talk so after an embrace like that? Confused, Myfanwy kept pace with his long strides, ignorant of what lay ahead, but knowing she needed his touch again. A strong hand in hers was not enough and never would be again.

"Arragh—?" she began, but he shook his head, raising a broad finger to his mouth.

"They may be near. No need to let them know where we are...yet."

She could not credit her brothers and their companions waited to do them harm but Arragh believed it. Just as her brothers were convinced Arragh was a monster. Surely no monster acted with such gentleness or offered such wild joy from his touch. If she could but tell her father and persuade Arragh...

"View, halloo!" The cry rose as she and Arragh ventured from the cover of the trees. Others took up the echo like a hunting party in full cry. Hounds bayed and Myfanwy glanced over her shoulder to see a racing mob approaching with her brothers at the head. "We have them!"

"Run!" Arragh commanded. Myfanwy's legs flew like a wild yearling's. Pumping her muscles, she raced beside the dragon, the cries of attack behind them and the clear wind in her face.

A cry came from behind. "The flame, loose the flame!"

"Faster!" Arragh urged, snaking his arm around her waist, forcing her to run at his pace.

Her lungs hurt, the blood pounded in her ears, her throat dry with effort. A tongue of flame roared at them. Arragh, ever alert, pulled Myfanwy to the left but she screamed with pain and stumbled. She'd have fallen but the dragon held her fast. Louder shouts came, one demanding more flame and stronger. Myfanwy wanted to call out to her brothers and the villagers that there was no need for force, no cause to fear Arragh, but pain raced through her leg and it took all her will not to falter.

How she ran on she never knew, Arragh's strength became hers. His arm held her to him and his legs ran for her. "Stay with me!" he gasped in her ear and with a bound that left her stomach behind, he lifted her off the ground. In a leap, they were eye level with the treetops. There was a sound like a branch breaking from an elm and they were aloft, scattering the birds in their path.

They were flying over the last trees in the glade, beyond the reach of the flames. An arrow, then three, sped past them but soon they were higher than any archer could reach, heading for the clouds.

Myfanwy glanced up, gasping between amazement and fear as she stared at Arragh's wings spread in a wide canopy of gray and green and gold. Stretched wider than two men's height, they moved gently as if ruffled by a summer breeze, but Myfanwy could feel the strength and power that moved them. Each gentle flutter of the great spread wings was matched by a slow ripple across his shoulders and chest.

If I were that strong, Myfanwy thought, *I need never fear anyone again.* But since she was soon to die, what matter was fear, or weakness, or the pain searing her leg? In the hands of her brothers or the dragon she was doomed.

But it was not unpleasant being doomed with Arragh's strong arm holding her close. Myfanwy rubbed her naked skin against the strange but pleasant texture of the dragon's skin.

"Why are you wriggling?" Arragh asked, his words faint as if lost in the wind.

"I can feel your skin."

Arragh looked down and smiled. "You will feel all of it before long, little one."

What did he mean? Rape her, he couldn't. She'd seen most clearly, he had no cock. Would he torture her? That she could not believe. Not with his arms holding her, and after the heat of his kiss. But what use did he have for her? Where were they going? Would she ever see her home and family again? Would—? She let out a quiet yelp as Arragh reached out his free arm toward her.

"I won't hurt you, Myfanwy, but you need to move. We have a long journey ahead and I'll fly more steadily without your weight to one side."

Without questioning, she grasped his free arm to bring herself even closer to his chest and the hard gray skin with its tracery of dark veins. The muscles of his arm shifted yet again.

25

Would he drop her? Was that how he killed his victims? But he'd promised not to hurt her! Her mind grappled with her fear and the confusion of the past minutes. "Sir...?" she began.

"Trust me, Myfanwy." She did. She was no doubt foolish and dragon-struck but she did trust Arragh. "Let me shift you." He moved easily until he held her flat against his broad chest. "Hold tight," he said.

Her arms met round his neck and he supported her back as she wrapped her legs round his waist. As she locked her ankles together, his hard dragon hide rubbed the soft insides of her thighs. She shuddered a little at the strange sensation but his arms held her, one hand cupping the back of her head, the other supporting her back.

She felt each finger of his spread hands and the strength of the arms that held her. Looking up, she could make out each mark on his chest and every curve of his face, but most of all, she felt the sweet abrasion of his skin against her legs. She was open, spread and vulnerable and Arragh held her as if he'd never part with her.

"Afraid?" he asked, his eyes still and questioning.

"Not as much as when the flame throwers hit me." Astonishingly, it was true. The scourge of the valley scared her less than her brothers and the villagers she'd known all her life.

Arragh frowned at her words. "They burned you?"

"My foot, as I ran."

The frown became a scowl. "They will suffer for that!"

"You promised not to molest the village."

"That was before they harmed you, Myfanwy." He glanced at her, his eyes softening a little. "Do you not want revenge on those who tried to kill you? Justice calls for it."

"I want no more killing."

"Who spoke of killing? Have you not yet realized I do not kill? My two earlier offerings were slain by your people's fire throwers, not by me."

That she understood. Now. Poor club-footed Mary could never have outrun the flames and timid Bron had no doubt been too scared to run. Maybe she had even fled toward the flame throwers, thinking she'd be rescued. That knowledge scrambled Myfanwy's thoughts. Was nothing as she'd believed? The dragon who was to have slain her, saved her. Her brothers, her one-time protectors, would have killed her. She shut her eyes to better sort out her confusion.

"You are in pain, Myfanwy?"

She looked up. A worry frown creased between Arragh's eyes. "A little."

"I think you lie, my sweet one. Flames always sear human flesh."

"I am in some pain, Arragh," she admitted, "but not as bad as I had feared." Where her leg and foot touched his back, his cool skin soothed the burn.

"I will ease it. Soon. Ahead is a high ledge we can use as a stopping place."

"We go far?"

"After I heal you."

How could he? They had nothing with them. Even herbalists needed their potions. But Arragh could outrun the flames and fly. Who knew what else he might do?

Lying back in the cradle of his arms, she became even more aware of her openness, with her legs spread wide around his bulk, and her breasts free in the breeze. It was improper, immodest, outrageous.

Her brothers would have killed at the thought that anyone would hold her so—and naked. Her brothers had tried to kill her.

Arragh had rescued her and now held her as if by right of possession. A right she had given and accepted when she agreed to leave with him. A right he'd claimed with one mind-bending kiss.

By the Goddess, what more would the dragon ask of her?

The fresh air helped cool her burning face, but not the fire inside her. Heat grew between her legs where she pressed against Arragh's smooth hide and her breasts seemed alive as the breeze brushed over them. She felt his hands on her bare back and wondered if she'd have sear marks from the heat in his fingers.

"Still in pain, Myfanwy?" Arragh asked, frowning.

"A little." Her foot and leg smarted, but other parts seemed more afire.

"Soon we can stop awhile and I will tend your hurt," he promised.

Myfanwy lay back in his arms, watched the scudding clouds overhead, and tried not to think what else Arragh might demand of her. Not that he'd asked much, other than she trust him and leave with him. She'd done the latter but felt a few qualms at the former. If she'd not been chosen as sacrifice, she'd have been wedded next spring to a man of her father's choosing, mistress of her own hall, and soon to bear children for her husband. Instead she was flying through the air to the far mountains, in the arms of the dragon of Cader Bala. Life did have its twists!

"You smile," Arragh said. "Why?" Barely hesitating, she told him her last thoughts. "You regret not having the young husband, and hall, and babes?"

"I don't know. It's hard to regret what one's never had. And since I expected to be dead by now..." Would be dead if not for Arragh. "One does not always find what one expects," she finished.

"Seldom," Arragh smiled. "I never thought to find you tied to the sacred oak."

She was about to ask him who or what he'd expected to find, but just then his hold tightened until she was flat tight against him. Her breasts all but flattened against his chest and with a sudden move Arragh and Myfanwy slowed, soared up a few yards and then dropped straight down. She'd have cried out but the fall took her breath away. Before she had time to think enough to worry, Arragh's feet hit ground, her legs released and he slid her down his body to stand facing him.

She stumbled with pain as her left foot touched rock. Arragh muttered what could only be a dragon oath, and swept her up in his arms. Three strides and they were at the rock face. Arragh set her down, her back against a boulder.

"Where are we?"

"In the western mountains," he replied. "There is nothing for us here. Once your foot is healed, we will go on."

Where? When? It would be weeks before her leg healed enough to walk on. The skin smarted and throbbed and one glance showed rising blisters and angry red flesh. Here there was nothing but rock and sparse ferns growing out of the cliff face. Behind Arragh's shoulders she glimpsed open sky, mist and clouds. She guessed they were hundreds, if not thousands of armspans above the ground. There was no sound but the wind, a lone bird cry, and the thudding of her heart. She shivered.

"Cold, Myfanwy?"

She should be, naked on a mountainside, but her body still held the heat of Arragh's closeness. "Not yet." But how long could she last, stranded here among rocks and stones?

"Let me look at your leg." Assuming consent, he knelt beside her, his knee brushing her thigh as his hands reached out and skimmed the livid flesh. "They should burn slowly for this." A low growl vibrated his chest. "We give them the gift of flame and this is how they abuse it!"

"You gave us fire?" Astonishment had her all but forgetting her pain.

Arragh nodded. "Many generations ago. The great Goddess taught us how to make fire and we chose to share the knowledge with humans. They were weak and naked then and we gave them the means of warmth and shelter. We shared other learning. We gave them the wheel and tools to build housing. We showed how to harvest the crops we taught them to grow. In some lands they still revere us for our knowledge and wisdom, but in your country, they resent our power. They try to kill us with flames, not realizing we cannot be destroyed by fire. We are of the mountains and will stand as long as the crags."

This was too much to absorb at one sitting, but she sensed there was more, much, much more. While she considered what to ask next, Arragh took her foot in one hand. The other smoothed over her smarting skin. "I'll heal your leg, Myfanwy. Be still, don't fight me."

As if she could, perched on a rock ledge too high for eagles to nest. As if she wanted to when both his hands circled just below her knee, above the first burn. His touch spread soothing warmth and cool pleasure all at once. She leaned back against the rough boulder, unaware of cold or space or distance, oblivious to everything but the confident touch of the dragon.

He moved slowly, applying a gentle pressure to her flesh, each fingertip a point of soothing coolness as heat fogged her mind. His hands slid down her leg by thumbspans, cooling the ache and easing the pain and causing wild heat in other places. Her breasts hung heavy and her nipples felt like the rocks at her back. His hands caressed her calf and another fire kindled deep between her legs. What was he doing? Was this the dragon fire her people feared so?

She'd agreed to not fight him, but now she was fighting her own body's wild response. What next? His hands were now on her ankle, the skin above soothed of all pain. She glanced down. All mark of burn was gone! Her flesh was clear and smooth as when she'd walked across the turf toward the edge of the trees. Was she dreaming? She'd heard travelers in the high mountains saw strange apparitions and visions in the thin air, but Arragh was no apparition. He was flesh and blood and dragon power.

His fingers cupped her heel as he lifted her foot. Warm, soothing breath washed like sweet balm over her skin. She knew nothing but the ten points where his fingers touched and the warm caress of his tongue on her instep. When her brothers tickled her feet, she'd screamed and hated it. Now, she purred like a cat in the sunshine. She leaned back against the hard rock and let sensation flood her, lost in a sweet unawareness until Arragh said, "It is well."

Her leg might be, but her body ached with needs beyond her understanding.

"Easy," Arragh said, rising and holding a hand out to her.

Glimpsing the sheer drop to the valley below went a long way to clearing her fuddled brain. "You've healed it!" Impossible! But he had. She did not feel the slightest twinge and no mark or scar remained. "How can that be?" she asked.

"We dragons have not shared all our knowledge with humans," he replied, a smile flashing as he spoke. "Come, Myfanwy, we must go on."

"To where?"

"Cader Ambris."

"The fire mountain?" Why not? Dragons were spawned in fire, or so the bards sang. "Is it safe?" Tales said demons and devils lived there. Tales also said her healer was a destroyer.

"With me, you will always be safe."

"I know." At that minute she did, and trusted him completely, even at the cliff's edge.

"Are you thirsty?"

She was. "Yes." And she was going to stay dry-mouthed. Where they'd find water on this windswept ledge the Goddess alone knew.

"Come." He held out his hand. Three short paces along the ledge he inclined his great head and pointed to a clump of fern growing from a cleft in the rock face. "After you, Myfanwy." Did he expect her to eat plants? If so, she would soon starve. His fingers were warm under her chin as he turned her face to his. "You don't know how?" he said, his green eyes flickering with amazement.

"How to do what?" Eat ferns?

His chuckle was slow and warmed her with its kindness. "Your people forget so much. Watch, I'll show you." An arm round her shoulders pulled her close. He pushed the fern aside with his free hand. They stood thigh to thigh and hip to hip, her skin soaking up his warmth against the wind. "Watch," he said and placed his mouth over the fern's fragile root.

His lips moved as if sucking deeply. Was he drawing moisture from bare rock? Yes! When he lifted his head after several minutes' slow drinking, a bead of clear mountain water hung from the middle of his lower lip. While she watched, his wide dark tongue gathered up the drop before it fell. "There's plenty left. The spring runs deep."

Completely baffled at how he'd drawn water from bare stone, but trusting he'd never lie, Myfanwy bent her head and rested her lips where his had marked the rock. Suck as she might, nothing came from the crevice but air and a damp dusting of earth. "There's no more there!" she said, lifting her lips and shaking her head.

Two fingers trailed like warm water down the side of her face. She almost forgot her thirst in the strange hunger his touch awakened. "You must draw it up, Myfanwy. Use your power."

"What power?"

His eyes darkened as he touched the same two fingers to the base of her neck and drew them down between her breasts to rest at the base of her breastbone. "The power within you, Myfanwy."

He would surely burn her skin with his heat. Hadn't the ropes that bound her fallen to the ground, charred and smoking from his touch? She had his word he'd never harm her. That she believed. But that she had power to summon water? Impossible! Not that she didn't need it to slake the fire rising deep within her.

His fingers still rested on her chest. Her rib cage rose and fell with each breath she took, and brushed the lower swell of her breast against his thumb. Soon all the water in the wide oceans wouldn't quench the heat inside her. "How can I?"

"Like this." His free hand gently pulled her head toward the rock. "Put your mouth right beside mine."

Her cheek pressed tightly against the hard bone of his jaw. Her chin rubbed the rough stone as he pressed her closer to the rock and she nervously opened her lips with his. The cold stone warmed to his touch. The corner of her mouth all but burned where it touched his. His jaw moved as he sucked and the soft click of his tongue in his mouth echoed beside her ear.

Water flowed, refreshing and icy cold, as if Arragh had tapped a hole in a cask of new mead. A steady stream of fresh water poured out the rock face. "Drink," Arragh said in her ear. "Drink deep, we cannot stop again."

Realizing the depth of her thirst, she sucked hard, gulping down the cool water as fast as it flowed into her mouth. Arragh's hand rested on her shoulder, a reminder of who now owned her life.

At last she slaked her thirst and lifted her head. Almost at once the flow became a thread-thin trickle, then dried up completely. Only a slightly flattened fern half-dislodged at the root showed where she and the dragon had drawn water from the mountain.

As she turned, Arragh's finger caught a dribble of water trailing down her chin. Warmth from his touch reached up to her lip. Then he offered her the last drop of water on his fingertip. "Never waste water. It's a gift from the Goddess."

Only half-hearing, she licked his finger, savoring the smoky taste of his skin and the rough edge of his retracted claw against her lip. A wild wish to feel his hands on her again called a whimper from her throat.

"Not yet." Arragh pulled his finger from her mouth. "Myfanwy, your needs must wait. We have miles to go yet, and the day is fading."

It was. The sun had sunk further in the sky even as they'd stopped on the ledge. She wanted to ask what he knew about her needs. But the expression on his face forestalled her questions. "I'm ready."

His great hands lifted her by her waist. Without being told, she put her arms round his neck. His hands slid down her back and as he angled her hips, she wrapped her legs around his waist. They hadn't spoken. She'd followed the directions of his hands and her instincts, settling her body comfortably against his.

Or she was comfortable until the hands cupping her buttocks tilted her closer. The soft skin of her thighs rubbed along the firm flesh round his waist. The soft, warm place between her legs made contact with the ridge that ran down his belly. Contact! It was as if he'd struck every bell in the tower and called the rivers of the land into full spate all at once. She let out an involuntary gasp before she caught her breath and looked up at Arragh.

He was smiling, grinning, a sly satisfied look in his twinkling eyes. "Myfanwy, we must go. Hold tight."

Hold tight! Her entire body was tight as a bowstring. Arragh was playing with her, that much she knew. And even more, she welcomed his games. How had she ever felt terrified at his sight? Why... That thought was lost as Arragh leaped off the ledge.

They dropped straight down, then pulled up as Myfanwy watched his wings unfurl like the sails on a great ship. With a shift of his shoulders, Arragh turned toward the setting sun, his strong wings carrying her away from home and toward the great fire mountain in the distant west.

Twilight came and still Arragh flew on without faltering. Darkness fell just as the light of the fire mountain approached, the warm glow turning the gloom golden. They were here!

Arragh had carried her all the way west to Cader Ambris. What awaited her now?

Chapter Three

They crossed the rim of the crater and dropped. This time she anticipated the fall. Moments later, Arragh stood on firm ground and lowered her down his body until she stood in front of him.

"Welcome to Cader Ambris, Myfanwy."

She smiled up at him, glad to be still at last. This was his territory—a fire mountain. She looked around the vast crater. Below them the land sloped gently for many leagues to the distant glowing heart of Cader Ambris. In the golden light she saw green swards, planted gardens, a road curving around the crater, and a cluster of moving figures approaching.

"There are others here!"

"Yes. Did you think I lived alone? They come to greet you."

"But..." she hesitated, suddenly aware of her nudity, "I have nothing to wear."

"Neither do they." He nodded toward the approaching crowd. "Your human rules belong in your world. Now you are in mine. We have no use for your trailing linens and woolen swathes. They prevent straight clear flight. Being my mate is all the cover you will ever need. If the winds are cold, I'll heat you until you learn to warm yourself."

She only half-heard what Arragh said. Her eyes were on the dragons who now stood in a semicircle around her. Some taller, some darker, in all shades of gray, some almost as pale as she felt, but not one gave her nakedness a glance.

"You brought her!" one said to Arragh.

"At last!" another said.

"I have," Arragh said, quietly enough that no one spoke for a minute. "I bring Myfanwy, daughter of Harwed Rees. Let all know I claim her. We are both weary from travel and must rest, but in the morning we will gather here."

Myfanwy shivered as he spoke. It wasn't over now that she'd arrived at Cader Ambris. It was just beginning. What waited in the morning? Would they throw her into the fire as sacrifice? Would the others tear her limb from limb as she'd once feared Arragh would do?

"Ease your worries, Myfanwy." Arragh's hand closed over her shoulder as he spoke. "I didn't bring you here for harm but to make you my mate."

"How can it..." she began. "How can we mate?" The thought didn't frighten, but it surely confused.

"I'll show you," he replied. "I will cherish you and teach you to summon the joy within you. There will be pleasure between us. Much more than our brief touching on the ledge." Blush flooded her face. It had been deliberate! "You are weary and hungry. You must rest because tomorrow I will give you very little. Go with them, they will take care of you and prepare you in the morning."

"Go with who?" There had to be twenty of them now and the prospect of being abandoned by him among a throng of dragons was terrifying. "Granned, Marbra, and Rarrp." As Arragh spoke three dragons came forward. They were shorter and slimmer than many of the others—women perhaps?

Looking at them there was no way to tell male from female. How could Arragh talk of mating? "Take Myfanwy with you," he went on. "Feed her, let her rest and in the morning, prepare her for me."

It sounded like being trussed and larded! But Arragh had promised no harm would ever befall her. Could she trust him? She had so far...

The three dragons nodded at Arragh. The one called Granned held out her hand. "Welcome, Myfanwy. We have waited so long for Arragh to bring a mate." She smiled and as Myfanwy smiled back, the others greeted her with a warmth that settled a few of Myfanwy's fears.

Without another word, they led Myfanwy along the road until they reached a tall opening in the rock. "You can rest in here," Rarrp said quietly. "Will you enter?"

Myfanwy paused just long enough to look back down the curving road. Arragh was watching, a dark silhouette in the gathering night. He raised an arm in salute. Myfanwy waved back before turning to the others and stepping through the dark opening.

Three or four paces through a narrow hallway and Myfanwy stepped into a wide, high-ceilinged room cut into the very side of the mountain itself. All four walls were smooth polished stone, as was the floor that was warm under her bare feet. Wide divans covered with furs stood in alcoves along the walls and in the center of the room was a table covered with food and drinking vessels.

But what surprised Myfanwy most of all was the light. The walls were solid rock, not even a chink of a window existed, but the room was as bright as a spring meadow at noon.

"Will you eat with us, Myfanwy?" Granned asked.

Myfanwy was hungry enough to gnaw chunks off the rock. But they were offering her more than ripe peaches or small round cheeses as yellow as sunshine. They were offering her friendship and sisterhood as they waited on her word. "With pleasure."

They pulled low stools up to the table. Marbra reached for a white ewer and filled matching goblets with dark red wine. "May you be content with us," she said raising her glass.

The others echoed and watched Myfanwy as she drank. The wine was rich and smooth and too heady on a stomach empty since yesterday. She was more than glad of the slices of crumbly yellow cheese and the soft flatbread Rarrp broke and shared with her.

"Will you be content to stay with us," Granned asked, "or will you wish to return to your own people?"

Marbra cast Granned a wary glance as if she'd spoken out of place. Rarrp made a sign as if to quiet her. Myfanwy looked at all three dragons.

"My people tried to kill me with Arragh. I do not think I can return…if I knew the way or could walk that far."

"Then you will stay?" Rarrp asked, as anxious as Granned. To cover her apparent confusion she passed Myfanwy a platter of dark purple grapes.

Myfanwy broke off a branchlet of seven grapes. "What else can I do?" She bit into one grape. It was sweet as honey gathered from jasmine flowers.

"Stay with us and make Arragh very content," Marbra said. "He has been alone too long."

"How long?"

"Since his first mate died of wasting." Marbra refilled Myfanwy's goblet. "The year after the Solwent froze."

Myfanwy's grandmother used to talk of the winter the Solwent froze! "How old is Arragh?"

"We're dragons," Granned said. "Time does not touch us in the crater of fire." She smiled at Myfanwy. "It will not touch you if you stay."

That thought was sobering, almost chilling. She'd better accustom herself to not being surprised at what she saw and heard in this land. She took another sip of the smooth wine and as she set her goblet down, ran her finger around the gilt band on the rim. "These goblets, they are thin as hammered silver, but they're not metal, are they?"

"White pottery," Rarrp replied with a smile. "The clay comes from far in the south and they are fired in the heat of the mountain."

This was pottery! Could anything be more different from the rough terra cotta vessels turned by the village potter? "It's so fine!"

Rarrp smiled, taking her words as praise. "I'm pleased you like them. I made you a set."

Silent for a moment, Myfanwy looked from the fine-rimmed goblet to Rarrp's anxious eyes. "I thank you, but..."

"When Arragh told us he was going east to seek another mate, we prepared gifts for you."

"I am honored to have such a gift, to have all your gifts. I thank you." Not sure what else to say and still very unsure of the next few hours, to say nothing of the morning and the future, Myfanwy downed the last wine in her glass, shaking her head when Marbra made to refill it. "This wine is too fine to drink deeply."

"And you are too weary to drink and eat much longer," Granned said. "Come, I will show you the bathing room so you may wash before you sleep."

What she needed was a privy!

Granned led Myfanwy through an opening into a dim room, pausing in the doorway to rest her hand on the wall. In an instant, sunshine lightened the darkness.

Myfanwy blinked at the light and stared in bewilderment. "What did you do?"

Now it was Granned's turn to be surprised. "Turned on the light."

"How?"

"By the switch in the wall." She demonstrated, pressing her fingers in a small indentation in the stone and then letting Myfanwy work the switch.

It was a wonder. At a finger's touch the dark became day. Arragh had mentioned the learning of the dragons but this... "But how does the light come?"

"As all light, from the sun. We store it and summon it when we need it." Granned spoke as if it was as simple as gathering nuts in autumn. "Just as we take the fire of the mountain to warm our homes and heat our stoves and water." As she spoke, she turned a small metal handle and warm water poured from the wall to a fine white basin. Rarrp's workmanship, Myfanwy didn't doubt. This was all so fine, but she still needed a privy or she would shame herself. How far was it to the outhouse?

It was under her feet. At least almost. Granned pointed out a low white basin in the corner of the room. It had ledges for her feet so she could squat and she showed Myfanwy the chute of water that cleansed the basin at the touch of a handle.

To relieve oneself indoors in the warmth with no need of a maid to empty the chamber pots amazed Myfanwy. But to wash in warm water that flowed from the wall at a touch, and then flowed away so no slops remained, was a marvel. She washed herself with the sweet-scented soap. She did wonder at the vast basin that filled one good third of the room. Could it be an enormous bathing tub? Why not? Seemed marvel after wonder awaited her here.

She thought briefly of Arragh. He had claimed her as his mate. A man of her father's choosing would have done no differently. But she would have half-known what to expect from a man—but from a dragon? She reached for the soft drying sheets on the rail, and found them warmed. They lived in warmth and comfort here, and now, so did she.

From habit she looked around for a sleeping shift but there was none, of course. No one here seemed shamed by nakedness, so she would not be.

Extinguishing the light with her fingers, Myfanwy walked back into the first chamber.

They had cleared the remnants of food from the table and pulled out the divans from the recesses in the walls.

"Your bed, Myfanwy," Marbra said as she drew back the fur cover of the closest.

Never had a bed been more welcome or so soft. Myfanwy gladly slipped between the soft sheets as Rarrp plumped the pillow and Granned kissed her good night.

Marbra settled the covers over Myfanwy's shoulders. "Sleep well, Myfanwy."

"Sweet dreams, dear human," Granned said.

"Sweet dreams of Arragh," Rarrp said with a twinkle in her eyes.

"And in the morning they will all come true," Marbra added.

Would they? Myfanwy shivered even under the ample covers. What did await her in the morning? She would see Arragh again and they would be mated. Virgin she might be but she hadn't lived nineteen years without knowing much went on

43

between men and women. What went on between dragons and women was anybody's guess!

He'd kissed her, true, and she'd gladly have more of those. He'd been gentle and kindly. What else could a wife hope for from her man? But what did a dragon ask of a mate? What would happen between them...in the morning?

Myfanwy tossed and lay awake despite her weariness, listening to the soft breathing of the dragons sleeping across the room. Then she heard the soft rustle of sheets and cautious footsteps across the room.

"Myfanwy?" a voice whispered.

It was Marbra. "Yes?"

"You can't sleep?"

"Not yet."

"You are lonely and unsure of the morning." Myfanwy nodded. "I understand." Marbra slid quietly under the sheets, her body warm and sweet-scented. "I will sleep beside you. Remember, you need never be alone among us."

Glad of the other woman's—no, dragon's—presence, Myfanwy slowly relaxed into sleep. But she had no dreams, not of Arragh or of her lost home.

Arragh stood on the rim of the fire mountain, the rising moon behind him, as he looked down at the glow deep in the heart of the crater, and the dark building to the right where Myfanwy slept with her attendants. Did she sleep or was she lying awake pondering on the morning? All he could think about was his brave and beautiful victim. He tossed his great head back and laughed aloud at the clouds. Victim she was not and never would be! Victims cowered. Myfanwy looked him in the eye, even when bound and helpless.

How she'd trusted him, running at his word, and letting him carry her away. When the sun rose, she would be prepared. Readied for their mating.

And a worthy mate she was, given she was human.

Arragh shook his head. What fools they were! Show them fire and they use it to destroy. Give then knives and they turn them into weapons. If they knew how to call water, they'd no doubt cause floods on purpose. They had so very little, and half of what they had, they misused. Dragons would share no more of the Goddess's knowledge with them. What humans needed or wished to learn they could find out for themselves, even if it took generations.

He had the one human worth having, and soon he would possess her utterly. His body quivered at the prospect, remembering how she'd wrapped her legs around him, opening herself completely. She'd shown passion when he'd rubbed himself against her clit. Tomorrow he'd have her screaming with joy.

The moon rose overhead, and finally Arragh flew down to stand outside the room where she slept. He waited there in the night quiet until he sensed another at his elbow. It was Grragh, his brother. Was he missing his mate, Granned, as she watched over Myfanwy?

"Are you sure about this?" Grragh asked.

"Yes," Arragh replied.

"It's too great a sacrifice."

Arragh smiled. "It will not be a sacrifice."

Chapter Four

Myfanwy woke slowly, her mind groggy from sleep as she lay under the furs, and let her thoughts coast back over the events of yesterday. Had it only been a day since her brothers had taken her to the grove and lashed her to the sacrificial oak? Her fears that morning were a lifetime away. Shouldn't she have new fears for this morning? But all she felt was nervousness at the unknown rituals ahead. Arragh had promised no harm would come to her and she trusted his word just as she trusted the sun to rise.

She snuggled under the covers, thinking of her groom to be. A dragon! Never when she'd talked with her girlhood companions about potential husbands had the possibility of a dragon even entered their minds. And in a few hours, she would mate with him. That perplexed her. Having now seen both male and female dragons, she saw no difference. Was mating between dragons different than men and women? Myfanwy shivered at the uncertain and unknown. She should not dwell on that, but she could not stop any more than she could forget how it felt with his great arms around her, the openness and vulnerability of riding him, her legs wide spread, or the wild pleasure she'd felt, rubbing herself against his hard dragon belly. If this was dragon mating, she hoped they would mate very soon.

Her face flushed at the thought. She was lusting after a dragon! How her father and brothers would denounce her for that. But they were far away beyond the great mountains and hadn't they given her to the dragon? She would do as a dutiful daughter should and go unprotesting to her dragon's bed...assuming he used a bed that is.

At her chuckle, Granned came into the room. "You're awake." She walked over to the bed and offered her hand. "Come, it will take time to get you ready."

"You should have woken me."

"No, you needed the rest. A long journey yesterday, and Arragh to please today." She grinned a teasing dragon grin, so like Myfanwy's cousin Blodwyn. "Come on." As she spoke, Granned tugged Myfanwy with one hand and pulled back the covers with the other.

Myfanwy braced herself for the cold rock under her bare feet but the floor was warm and the air about her felt more like summer than a chamber deep in the earth. She followed Granned into the adjoining room. The deep basin Myfanwy noticed last night was filled with scented, steaming water and Marbra and Rarrp waited on the edge, feet dangling and stacks of fresh folded drying sheets beside them.

"Come join us!" they said as they slid off the side into the basin.

With only a second's hesitation, Myfanwy eased herself into the water and sat with the others on the broad ledge that served as a bench. Myfanwy leaned back against the smooth rim and closed her eyes a few minutes. This was close to sinful! Warm scented water up to her chin, and a bathing tub big enough to stretch and move around in. And she'd once thought bathing in a wooden tub a luxury.

Rarrp handed her a cake of soap scented with rose petals, and Marbra offered her a soft yellow sponge. "Would you have us wash you?" she asked.

Myfanwy shook her head. "I thank you, but no!" That was approaching decadence.

But the others did not think so. They soaped each other's backs and legs, laughing and splashing until Myfanwy tossed useless propriety aside and joined Granned in soaping Marbra's back. As she worked her fingers through the scented foam, Myfanwy couldn't help noticing that each woman's skin was a different shade of gray. Marbra was closest to Arragh, Granned was pale as the inside of a field orchid and Rarrp was almost the same blue-gray as the pebbles found by the river at home. But none of them had wings like Arragh. "Why don't you have wings?" Myfanwy asked and blushed, fearing her question might offend.

It didn't.

"We do," Marbra said. "We're dragons."

"Why would we need them indoors?" Granned asked.

It was Rarrp who made the best sense. "You don't understand, do you?" She smiled as Myfanwy shook her head in confusion. "We shape shift. When we need wings, we have them. If not, we don't. They'd get in the way indoors."

Myfanwy felt her mouth drop in surprise. "You shape shift? You change?"

"It's part of being dragon," Granned explained. "When we need strength or to fly, dragon is the best shape. For speed on land, great cats or deer are faster. By sea, we take dolphin shape." She shrugged. "And sometimes, of necessity, we appear as human."

"But why?" Myfanwy was almost too amazed to think.

"So we can travel the world ànd see what you humans have made of it," Rarrp replied.

"Which isn't very much!" Granned said. "You humans often abuse the knowledge we share."

"I'm sorry..." Myfanwy began, remembering what Arragh told her about fire, "but many of us did not know these were gifts from...dragons." Her mind still spun at the thought.

Marbra sighed. "That is what saddens us."

"Enough," Rarrp said. "We're not here to lay the faults of humans on Myfanwy's shoulders. We have to prepare her for Arragh and if we delay, we'll surely hear him roar!" She leapt out of the bathing pool and reached for two of the drying sheets. One she tossed over her own broad shoulders and the other she held for Myfanwy.

"We'll have to take care of your hair," Rarrp said as Myfanwy toweled it dry.

Myfanwy paused. After Arrgh's cutting there wasn't much left. She looked at the three women's hairless heads, and Rarrp's meaning hit her. "You mean cut it all off."

Marbra shook her head. "No, remove it. You belong among dragons now. We only have hair when we shift." She made having hair sound like the great pox.

Wrapping her in a heated sheet, they settled Myfanwy on a bed of pillows by the smaller basin. Marbra rubbed a sweet-smelling paste on Myfanwy's head while Rarrp brought her a goblet of honey-sweetened juice, tasting of ripe peaches freshly gathered on a summer's day.

Rarrp refilled the goblet twice before Marbra decided it was time to rinse off the paste. They had Myfanwy lean over the basin and Granned rinsed her with a strange pipe that spewed a rain of warm water. The stream washed away the paste and all Myfanwy's hair with it. Even her eyebrows were gone! She ran her hands over her now-bald head. Odd was not the word for how the smooth skin felt under her hands. Her brothers would have turned away in shock and considered her shamed but here it would help her look like the others...the dragons.

"Now your arms," Granned said. Rarrp held Myfanwy's arms over her head as Marbra used the same sweet mixture on her armpits. That took only a few minutes. Depilating Myfanwy's legs took much longer. They held them up, stretched them out and then had Myfanwy turn onto her belly, so even the backs of her legs and thighs were left smooth as a baby's.

"Is this really necessary?" Myfanwy asked as Marbra spread the sweet unguent on the insides of the thighs.

"Of course," Granned said. "You cannot go to Arragh with hair on your body."

Myfanwy was dangling her legs over the bathing basin as Rarrp and Granned rinsed when the significance of that struck her. "All my hair? Even on my quim?"

"Especially that on your quim," Marbra said.

"You can't think to offer yourself to Arragh with hair," Granned sounded horrified.

Put that way... "If it is necessary," Myfanwy conceded.

"It is," Rarrp added with almost a sigh. "We must prepare you completely."

And they did. While Myfanwy lay on her back, legs spread and feet flat on the soft pillows, she tried not to think of the immodesty, the indecency of so displaying her body to others. Her face burned scarlet and her knees shook.

"Be unafraid," Granned said, stroking Myfanwy's smooth head. "Marbra will use a soothing potion on your quim. It will not hurt."

Hurt had been the least of her concerns. But now that it had been mentioned. "How do you know it won't?"

Marbra turned, a small polished pot in her hand. "It's what we use on ourselves!"

At that Myfanwy sat straight up. "You have hair?" She looked at the three of them, smooth-skinned and shining.

"We would if we didn't take care of it," Granned replied. "Not as much as you humans but we grow a little on our backs and groins. We take it off as soon as it shows." Her tone of voice implied that not removing it was unclean. Maybe it was...to dragons.

And she was about to be mated to one.

Myfanwy nodded. "I see." She did. Without a word, she slid back flat on the pillows and spread her legs.

Marbra's touch was gentle and confident. In moments, the scented lotion covered Myfanwy's pubes and she tried her best to relax as she waited the necessary time before rinsing off.

"Your sex is such a beautiful shade of pink, like wild roses." Sitting cross-legged between Myfanwy's knees, Marbra spoke as casually as if she was admiring a new sash or a fresh hair ribbon.

Myfanwy stifled a gasp. Her face had to be the color of autumn sage blooms!

"You're right!" Granned stepped closer and peered over Marbra's shoulder. "It's beautiful, so delicate."

"Let me see!" Rarrp jumped up and joined the others.

Myfanwy wanted to sink between the pillows and disappear. This was impossible, to be stared at while so lewdly spread, to be talked about in such a way!

"Myfanwy," Granned sounded worried. "What's the matter? You look distressed."

Distressed wasn't the word! But one look at the concern in the dragon's dark eyes and Myfanwy bit back her instinctive sharp response. She exhaled slowly. "Among my people, we do not comment on each other's womanly parts."

Now it was their turn to be amazed.

Granned showed how a dragon's jaw dropped. "Why not?"

"What a shame," Rarrp said, "to not admire such beauty."

"Human ways are different," said Marbra, a clear note of regret in her voice. She smiled at Myfanwy from between her knees. "Without doubt, Arragh will admire you and give you immense pleasure."

After those few minutes on the ledge, Myfanwy didn't doubt it.

Granned sighed. "What a mistake to ignore something so lovely, but..."

"You look at each other's?" Myfanwy had to ask but almost choked as the words came out.

"Yes." Rarrp couldn't seem to hide her amusement. "If we wish."

"How are you different? Aren't you pink?" Had she really asked that? Yes, and without a trace of concern, Rarrp propped a foot on the edge of the washing basin and parted the outer folds of her vulva. Her inner skin was pale, like the lining of an oyster shell. "Are all dragons like that?" Heaven help her. What was she asking?

Nothing that surprised a dragon.

"Mostly," Granned replied and proceeded to show that her inner lips were a little darker than Rarrp's.

Marbra's were even paler still, like a marten's fur in winter.

Displaying one's body's hidden places was as unremarkable as nudity in this land of dragons. Perhaps she should ask about how she and Arragh would mate. But even as she thought it, she knew she couldn't...or could she? It seemed...

"Oh," Marbra said, as if remembering what they should be doing. "Time to rinse, Myfanwy."

Her short curls washed away with the last of the sweet-smelling lotion. Myfanwy stared at her depilated body. She did look different. She felt different. Perhaps removing her woman's hair peeled away the remains of her old inhibitions. After studying the soft planes of her vulva and her now-naked cleft, it was little discomfort to lie on her belly, while Granned and Rarrp held apart the two globes of her buttocks and Marbra removed the last vestiges of hair from Myfanwy's body.

They'd refilled the large bathing basin with warm water and this time Myfanwy slid into it as easily as the others. But this time, as she moved, the feel of warm water on her most secret places sent strange thrills rippling through her body. Turning her hips and stretching out one leg only increased sensation. A little jump and landing with a splash shot a tremor deep inside and spreading her legs and squatting slowly caused a rush of sensation that had her catching her breath.

"You're pleased," Granned said, giving a teasing smile.

"Yes."

It wasn't just the water, even the touch of the drying sheets stimulated nerve endings she never knew existed. Until she came to this world inside the volcano.

Tossing aside the used drying sheets, they led Myfanwy to a divan and as she stretched out on her belly, massaged her with rose-scented oil. Their practiced hands eased each knot of tension in her body, working and soothing until Myfanwy was half-asleep and it seemed her bones hung loose in her body. Her breathing slowed and her muscles felt liquid. They turned her over and worked the last traces of strain from her legs and arms and soothed the tightness in her head and face. When they were finished, Myfanwy was amazed she could still stand. She felt loose and supple and spry enough to fly herself if need be.

But they weren't finished. They gave her more fruit nectar to drink, this time flavored so intensely with raspberries, Myfanwy fancied she could taste the sun in each sip. They anointed her body with a soft cream until her skin gleamed and sprinkled her with flakes of gold so she glistened in the light like gold-veined marble. But marble was cold to the touch and Myfanwy felt her body pulsing with heat and life and a need she only half-understood.

"One last thing." Rarrp stepped up with a gold-tipped brush in one hand and a saucer in the other and Myfanwy watched in silent fascination as her nipples were gilded. They went hard at the touch of the soft brush and seemed almost to preen as Rarrp finished decorating the aureoles. "Spread your legs," Rarrp said and expertly decorated Myfanwy's slit with twin lines of gold that joined at the tip of her sex lips to swirl an inch or so below her navel.

Myfanwy gasped. This was her body that gleamed and shone and instead of the shame and humiliation she'd been taught to feel naked, she gloried in the change.

"It's time!" Rarrp said and kissed her. "Your mate is waiting."

Myfanwy swallowed. Arragh was outside. A tremor of anticipation gathered in her groin. She was about to meet him. To mate with him. Her throat tightened. Could she? Could she not? She had given her word as the daughter of Harwed Rees. There was no going back.

"I'm ready." Her voice sounded tight and hoarse, but her mind was as easy as her relaxed muscles.

"Go then." Marbra kissed her on the cheek and led her back through the hallway she'd entered the night before. Only one short night? It seemed like a lifetime away.

Granned and Rarrp embraced her and as she neared the opening, stepped back.

"Go," Granned said as Myfanwy hesitated. "Arragh waits. When you step out the doorway, don't hesitate, walk straight toward Arragh."

"You're not coming?" Myfanwy turned in panic. In a few hours, these women had become friends, her link to her new future.

"To meet your mate?" Rarrp seemed caught between shock and amusement.

"We stay behind. You don't." Marbra gave her a gentle nudge.

So, she had to go on alone. She could. She'd been alone in the sacred grove and then she feared death. Now a far, far better fate awaited her. One pace from the opening, Myfanwy looked over her shoulder. "I thank you," she said, feeling an odd sadness at leaving these women, and turned and stepped out into the sunshine.

Her skin glinted and glimmered in the light but she barely noticed. Arragh took all her attention. He gleamed brighter than the sun, standing with great wings outspread, wings of dazzling gold. There were other dragons watching but she scarcely noticed them. All she knew was Arragh, her intended. Arragh who brought her here over the great mountains, golden Arragh magnificent as the sun. Her heart fluttered inside her ribs. Her dry throat tightened even more as she stepped forward. Her stomach did a little flip with the next step and then her legs moved on their own. She no longer walked. All dignity or ceremony aside, she ran toward her golden mate.

Did others feel this seeing their readied mate? Every fiber in his dragon's body tightened at the sight of Myfanwy—his Myfanwy, his mate—as she stepped from the doorway and hesitated a moment in the light.

At his very first sight of her, in the gloom of that glade, he sensed beauty under the hair and cloth that covered her. Removing that useless shift, he'd been rewarded with pearly soft skin and sweet white breasts, but now, adorned and prepared as a female should be, she was stupendous.

It was as if the heat from the mountain's core burned inside his chest. This shining mortal was his! In minutes he would take her in his arms and carry her off to the mating pavilion. Dear Goddess. Wild longing to possess roared inside him as she took two steps closer. Her eyes widened at the sight of the assembly but she came on, unflinching and unafraid. And he'd feared the sight of the entire community of dragons would unnerve her. She approached them with dignity and poise, or did until she started running toward him, her arms wide open as his heart. He half-expected to burst with the pride. Instead a wild surge of desire all but took his control.

"Arragh!" she cried, as she ran into his arms.

He caught her round the waist and lifted her off her feet. Holding her aloft, he tasted each gilded nipple and watched the response that rippled down to her belly. She was his. Utterly and completely.

"Myfanwy," he said setting her on her feet. "Come."

How she trusted him! She took his hand and without question stepped up to stand beside him. Only then did she look around, her eyes wide as if seeing the assembled crowd for the first time.

"There are so many," she whispered.

"Not as many as there once were," he replied. This was no time to tell her every last one of them prayed she would alter that. That her human womb would bear healthy young whelps.

"Oh," she replied. "Will you..."

The first notes of the anthem drowned her question. Her face lit with amazement and her eyes shone with wonder as the voices blended and the chorus echoed off the sides of the crater. Poor bereft human, to live this long and never have heard the beauty of dragon melodies.

How had this creature of courage and beauty come from those peasants who misused and devalued the gifts they were given? As if it mattered! Myfanwy was his and that was all he cared to know. As the singers began the second verse, Arragh led her on the slow promenade around the semi-circle of singers that everyone might see his chosen mate up close. The future of the dragons.

She walked carefully, still unsure of herself it seemed. That intrigued many of the onlookers. Demure was not a word often used to describe females here. But Myfanwy met smiles with smiles, and when they reached where Granned, Rarrp and Marbra stood, she left his side to embrace them like sisters.

It seemed she had fascinated Grragh's mate and her companions too.

"Come, Myfanwy," Arragh said. She turned at once, stopping just to give Marbra a final embrace.

"Yes?" Myfanwy asked, a question in her voice.

"Time to leave," he said and gathered her in his arms.

With a laugh, she wrapped her arms around his neck. "Where are we going?"

"To the mating pavilion." Before she could ask another question, he launched himself in the air.

Chapter Five

Her heart raced so, it surely out-paced Arragh's great gilded wings. She was being carried off by a dragon and had never in her life felt so cherished. Myfanwy leaned her head against his gray-veined chest and listened to the beating of his heart, like a deep echoing drum sounding its own rhythm. "You are mine! You are mine!" it seemed to pulse in her ear.

She was. His. Taken from her village. Flown over the western mountains. Swept across the crater of the great volcano—to their mating. She gasped with surprise as they rose several manspans on a gust of warm air and then dropped.

Arragh barely noticed, his wings beat on and he never wavered from his course. "We just crossed the heart of the mountain," he said, his breath warm on her bare scalp. "Halfway there."

Her heart skittered inside her chest. Just minutes away. She looked down at her body reclining in his arms, nipples shining like ducats, her naked quim lewdly edged with gold, and the smooth line sweeping up her belly to form a curlicue. Hers surely was a different body from the one that waited in fear in the grove and in a few hours, she'd be another woman still.

They dropped in a rush, a greensward coming up to meet them, but Arragh landed softly, his great legs taking the jolt. "We're here, Myfanwy," he said as he set her on her feet.

They were standing on close-cropped grass, the soil warm under her toes, the air around them still. The green lawn sloped toward a high stone wall that enclosed them. A solid wall with no door or gate. A wall that blocked out the world, secluded them. Arragh's hand curled round her shoulder. She rested her hand atop his and slowly met his eyes.

They were deep, dark green with blue lights. She read in them need and longing, and a fleeting emotion that seemed like uncertainty but it couldn't be...or could it?

"Is this where we stay?" she asked.

Arragh nodded. "Do you want to walk?"

She wanted to fly—to safety. But watching the emotions flickering across his face, she knew she'd be safer nowhere in the world than here with Arragh. "Yes," she replied.

Hand in hand, they strolled the wide grass paths between hedges of lavender and beds of roses. The garden was planted with a riot of scented plants, mignonettes spilled over stocks, carnations grew between hyacinths and spring narcissi. Purple and white lilacs blossomed in one corner and wisteria and jasmine tumbled over the walks. Flowers of all seasons bloomed together as if in disregard of the calendar, or maybe all months were one here in the dragon's roost.

"Arragh," she asked as they paused by a small waterfall, a warm waterfall she discovered as she trailed her fingers through the clear water. "Arragh," she repeated, "why did you bring me here?"

His heart all but spluttered out. He blinked a minute as if to erase all trace of her words from his mind. To no avail. When he opened his eyes, she was watching, waiting, and the echo of her question hovered between them. "This is the mating pavilion, Myfanwy. We dragons bring our mates here." The hurt in her eyes cut him to the quick. One glance told him that truth that evaded an answer was no better than prevarication. "You want to know why you are here with me?"

"Yes."

He had no choice but tell her the whole truth—and risk her censure, her anger, or the Goddess help him, her rejection. "I need you, Myfanwy. We all need you." Her eyes acknowledged the urgent tone of his voice, but gave away nothing else. He sat down on a raised bench covered with sweet-scented woodruff and looked up at the woman who held his hopes and the future of the race in her hands. "Myfanwy, once we roamed the earth as the first creatures. Now all that remains of the mighty dragons lives here in the mountain while you humans populate the earth and shape it to your will—building bridges, cutting roads across mountains, mining the riches from the depths. We don't begrudge you that, we held sway for millions of years, now is the age of the humans.

"But..." He paused, looking over the high walls across the crater where the others waited—and hoped. "We have become barren while you humans prosper and multiply. There have been no young ones in living memory." Arragh turned back to Myfanwy. "I hope, we hope, that you will bear me young."

"Can this be?" Her eyes were perplexed, not affronted.

"I don't know," he replied. "We can but hope." He wanted to touch her, to reassure her, to reassure himself, but wasn't sure he dared. Not now.

Her breasts rose and fell as she inhaled deeply and exhaled slowly. "And if I prove as barren as a...dragon. What will you do?" She held her arms still but her fingers twisted together and one square-shaped white tooth bit on her lower lip.

He couldn't keep his distance. It was impossible! "Listen to me, Myfanwy, and listen well. We dragons mate for life. Whatever does or does not come of our mating, nothing will separate us. Unless..." he paused knowing he had to say this, "you wish to return to your village, but I'm not sure how they will receive you now."

"I am." A frown creased between her eyebrows. "They would never take me back. They'd see me tainted by you, and stone me if they didn't burn me as unclean." What had he done to her? "You have me, Arragh." A hesitant smile turned up the corners of her mouth. "I hope and pray I am not barren."

That no longer mattered! That she was his was all he cared about. His heart swelled with a wild surge of triumph. He stepped closer. So did she. Her knees bumped just below his. He willed his to stay strong, not falter with his anxiety. He'd asked too much of her and she offered even more. He slid one hand down the soft warmth of her back. Pausing between her shoulder blades before easing his fingers over the soft skin and the delicate ridges of her spine. Finding the hollow at the small of her back, he splayed that hand to steady her against him and gently cupped her head with the other.

Her skull fitted into his hand like an acorn in its cap. She was so beautiful freed of the great mane of animal hair. His fingers explored the sweet bumps and creases of her skull. He kissed the smooth pale skin, feeling her warmth against his lips, tasting the freshness of her skin with the tip of his tongue.

He couldn't stop, not now that she'd offered herself. He covered the dome of her head with gentle kisses until he felt the tension ease from her body. As she leaned against him, he planted a slow kiss on her forehead. He lifted his lips away as she looked up—and smiled.

What more invitation could she offer than parted warm lips and a gleam of desire in her gray eyes? Heart tight and mind racing, Arragh lowered his mouth to hers. Her lips were sweet with promise as he touched them as softly as he knew how. He had to remember she was human and virgin, Myfanwy needed slow awakening to reach her full passion.

He gave her a series of soft, closed-mouth kisses. Each time he pursed his lips on hers, he pressed gently and released almost at once, pausing a second between kisses. It didn't take her long to pick up his rhythm. Soon she puckered her lips to meet his, her will and her need sweetening each kiss. He slowed his pace, making each touch longer and a wee bit stronger until there was more kiss than pause and Myfanwy filled the gaps with sighs. He slowed even more, but now when their mouths met, he applied more pressure until her lips opened softly like a flower in the sun, and she held her breath waiting for him to guide her.

He led. Gingerly. Shaping his dragon tongue small and narrow, he entered her mouth, marking it as his and his alone. She whimpered with need as he touched the tip of her tongue. Warmed by her response, he kissed deeper, exploring her mouth, caressing her until her tongue came alive under his. Now she pushed and pressed, urging him deeper until he widened his tongue to all but encompass hers. Still she gave, now seeking his mouth and melting against him as sexual curiosity stirred a fire under her skin.

Cupping the back of her head to hold her just where he wanted her, he eased his other hand over the roundness of her hip and up to caress the full curve of her breast. Every nerve in her body tensed, she let out a slow sigh and then heat rushed over her skin. He felt it in every inch of her. She was burning with need for him and what he could give her. She was hot with wanting.

"Arragh!" It came out half-sigh, half-moan. She pulled her mouth from his and tilted her head back to look up.

Her eyes gleamed with need. Her swollen lips quivered as if demanding to be kissed again and again and again. Her chest heaved and a soft sheen of perspiration glistened on her upper lip. Arragh tightened his touch on her breast, squeezing and slowly easing in rhythm with her hastened breathing. "You are mine," he said, whispering the words into her lips before he took her mouth again.

This time he pressed her mouth open and drove into her. His tongue the same size as before, but he moved harder and faster, wanting her to taste his need and awaken to her own passion. His hand tightened on her breast, his fingers played with her hard nipple as his lips worked her mouth.

She met his fire with heat, and his need with wanting. She took his kisses and returned them with greater ardor. As his hands skimmed over her body, she curved herself to his touch as if begging for his caress.

"Myfanwy, come!" Gathering her up in his arms, he strode toward the shelter carved into the side of the mountain.

Myfanwy looked up at her dragon mate and let out a slow, contented sigh. Was it possible to feel limp and energized at once? Yes!

"Pleased with yourself, wench?" Arragh asked, his eyes twinkling and amusement in his deep voice.

"Very!" Reclining in his strong arms, she grinned at him. "I think, too..." she ran the pad of her finger over the markings on his chest, "that you are very pleased with me."

The muscles in his belly and chest rippled with the laugh he tried to hold back. "I am, am I?"

"Yes." She could tell that much by the look in his eyes and the smile he couldn't hold back. "You are and I'm so glad." She

63

leaned against him, inhaling the sweet, smoky scent of his body and listening to his heart thrumming inside his wide chest.

A strange fluttering of expectation woke deep in her belly, radiating through every nerve and cell. She shivered with the awareness that each step Arragh took toward the rock doorway brought her closer to a life change from which she'd never be the same.

"Cold, Myfanwy?" he asked as a second shiver skimmed through her.

Cold? Never! A fire kindled between her legs and where Arragh's skin brushed hers, she burned with a need she didn't understand but instinctively wanted to. She longed to learn the secrets of her body and taste of the never spoken knowledge between a woman and...a dragon. She let her breath out slowly, only half-aware she'd been holding it. "Arragh..." she began but broke off as she fumbled for the words to express her excitement—and her anxieties.

"I know." Blue lights glinted in the depths of his dark green eyes. Her stomach clenched harder as he stepped over the threshold and strode confidently across the polished stone floor before sitting down on a low divan.

She was seated on his lap, her legs stretched out on the fur covers, leaning back on his arm and the pillows piled behind her. The room was warm, redolent with a heavy scent of spice and cedar. The pillows behind her back felt like silk. Arragh's skin rubbed with the teasing and now-familiar roughness. It seemed as if every hair of the furs brushed her legs in a separate motion. Her mind absorbed a maelstrom of sensations. She could hear the air around her, almost taste Arragh's heartbeat, and smell her own pulse echoing in her ears. She shivered as her senses all but overwhelmed her mind.

His fingertips trailed over one breast. She couldn't help the little whimper. She wanted his touch everywhere. His hand moved, slowly, surely, tracing soft figure eights around her breasts. The heat in his fingers shimmered down her body to the now-aching spot between her legs. As Arragh continued his slow caress, his palm brushed her nipples. They were pebble-hard now, that she could tell, hard and throbbing with need.

Myfanwy glanced down at her spread body. The same fingers that burned rope and linen gave pleasure as they danced over her pale skin, gray on white, like shadows cast on white marble. As he circled below her breasts, he trailed his fingers toward her navel, skimming her skin with a gentleness that intensified each touch. She was attuned to every breath he took and every pulse beat of her heart. Her body seemed heavy but alive with an unfamiliar energy. She closed her eyes as her head sank back on the pillows. Her legs fell apart and her shoulders went slack but her soul was on edge for whatever followed.

"Tell me what pleases you, Myfanwy. What do you want me to do?"

Her eyes shot open in surprise. "Arragh?"

"Tell me," he persisted, "what you like. I need to know."

"I like you touching me."

"How? Like this?" The pad of his thumb flicked her nipple, wringing a little cry from her. "Or this?" One warm finger traced a line between her breasts down her chest and lower. Pausing only when he reached the designs of gold just above her slit. But he didn't stop—with gentle pressure, he made small circles in her flesh.

She sighed. He increased speed and force until she moaned. Her body took on a life of its own. She had two pulses beating. One in her heart and one deep inside her quim that throbbed and grew until a wild moan spilled from deep inside her throat. Her hips rocked and shifted, reaching up to him, wanting more, needing more. "Arragh," she moaned.

"Yes, sweet mate." His finger slowed. "That pleases you?" She answered with a weak moan and a jerk of her hips. "Speak to me, Myfanwy." His finger stilled and the flat of his hand covered her belly, holding her down. "Tell me what you want."

"I don't know!" she half-cried in her bewilderment.

He planted a slow kiss at the base of her breastbone and looked up at her face. "What do you do to pleasure yourself?"

"Pleasure myself?" she repeated. What did he mean?

Now he looked confused. "When you pleasure your body. Give yourself sexual release. How do you touch yourself? Show me."

His meaning hit her. "You mean self-abuse! I would never! It's a sin. To do so merits severe punishment."

Now it was his turn to speak with shock. "How could they punish for that?"

"The leaders do. My cousin Gwenda was punished. She wore leaden mittens for weeks..." Myfanwy shook her head, remembering the shame and pain on Gwenda's face when she was accused before the village.

Arragh let out a soft growl. "How could your people so pervert the Goddess's greatest gift?" He shook his head. "Never forget, Myfanwy, your body is for joy and pleasure, as is mine. However we choose to take our pleasure and release is fitting."

The idea was shocking—and wonderful. "There is joy and pleasure in your hands. Will you touch me again?" she asked.

"Yes," he replied and lifted her to her feet. He stood with her. "Come," he said, taking her hand. "I will show you many ways to take pleasure."

Chapter Six

Wonder of wonders! Her legs not only supported her, but she could still place one foot in front of the other and walk as Arragh led her into the adjoining room—another bathing chamber. Both hands spanning her waist, he paused at the edge of the already-filled basin. Sweet scents of jasmine and lavender rose from the warm water. "We'll let the water pleasure us, Myfanwy!" he said and jumped.

Warm water splashed in her eyes, trickling down her face and neck. Arragh cupped his hands and poured more water over her. She reached up, from habit, to brush the hair from her face, and remembered it was long gone. Her body was now adorned in strange ways that pleased her mate but... "Arragh, won't the water wash away my gilding?"

"Myfanwy, that is dragon gold. Water will not remove it." He paused, his hand on the side of her face. "I will when I kiss it off."

Her stomach and heart clenched and flipped in opposite directions. Her nipples, yes she wished, hoped he would kiss her breasts again...but to kiss her slit? Her heart raced and her face flushed hot with the wicked joy at the prospect. "I think I will like that," she whispered.

"I'll make sure you do." His hand trailed down the side of her face and across her chin, one finger outlining her lips.

Emboldened by need and arousal, Myfanwy licked his fingertip, drawing it between her lips. He smiled. That was all the encouragement she sought. She sucked him in deeper until the first two joints of his long finger were deep within her mouth. She curled her tongue around him, tracing the knobs and creases of his skin, fluttering the tip of her tongue against his fingertip, finding a small crease under the nail, and a rough ridge along the top. She wanted to taste his all, to feel the very heat that loosed her bonds and freed her of her clothes. She needed everything and more. She ached to know the secrets of Arragh.

"Slow down, little one." Arragh eased his finger from between her lips. "Did that please you?" he asked as her lips parted in loss.

"Yes." Why, she didn't understand, but the slow thrills still thumped deep inside.

"It pleased me too, Myfanwy, but now, let me show you something else." His hands closed round her waist. "Open your legs and let them trail behind you."

Swimming in the lake by the village had never been like this! Arragh's touch and the sheer delight of warm water on her naked body were each a pleasure—but together! How she gloried in the wash of sensations. Opening her legs wider, she sighed with joy as the heat slowly rekindled between her legs. She stretched as flat as she could, so her breasts submerged and cut a swath through the water as he pulled her along. His grasp relaxed and now her hands just rested in his.

She slipped his hold and went under. Hearing his cry of surprise, she dived deeper. She was tempted to pull his legs from under him but they seemed planted as firmly as a hundred-year oak. Instead, she swam between them, surfacing a few yards behind him.

"Playing games, are you?" he asked.

"Yes!" She kicked sideways, propelling herself away as he lunged. It won her a few seconds, but no more. He was after her and caught her legs, but instead of pulling her under as she expected, he swam alongside and kissed between her shoulders as his hand closed on her breast.

A little wobbly, she stood, his arm round her shoulder now and his face very close to hers. "Let's play," he said and grabbing her hand, kicked off, pulling her after him.

Like a pair of otters, they played. Splashing and kicking from end to end of the ample bathing basin until Arragh finally scooped her up in his arms and leapt out. He set her on her feet and wrapped her in a warm drying sheet as the water ran off his shoulders and down his legs to pool by his feet. Myfanwy poked an arm through the folds of the sheet and ran her hands over his damp skin and the rivulets of water streaming down his chest. His hard, smooth skin was becoming familiar, less strange each time she touched him. Arragh was her dragon, her mate and soon... Her heart skittered at the thought of what soon awaited. It wasn't fear that caused the tightening in her belly. Could it be desire? Desire for a beast? Her throat tightened at the thought.

"What is it, little one?" Arragh patted her skin with the cloth and drew her close. "Afraid?"

Denial came almost as a reflex, but the concern in his eyes stopped her. "A little."

He wrapped the sheet tighter around her and pulled her closer. "Don't be." She couldn't miss the entreaty in his voice. "Myfanwy, I'll never hurt you. With me, you'll always be safe."

"I know," she replied without thinking. Minutes later, she couldn't think. Arragh's lips sent her brain in a whirl and her body wild for more.

He carried her the few feet to a low divan and tumbled her onto the pillows. She lay back and looked up at him. Her limbs went limp and her heart seemed to slow as Arragh placed one knee on the divan. Leaning over her, he slowly spread her legs, his fingers warm on her water-softened skin but nowhere near as warm as the heat gathering between her legs. She was open, exposed, her feet dangling and slow tendrils of heat reaching out from the tips of his fingers across her awakening body.

The divan dipped a little under his weight as he sat, so close that his hip brushed her side. A smooth hand spanned her belly and surely, confidently, moved upward to rest under the swell of her breasts. She anticipated the slow pressure on her flesh and the soft brushing of his thumb over her nipples. Her breath quickened and her heart sped as she lay back and let the wild sensations invade her body. How did a touch on her breasts stoke such heat between her legs? Why did a brush over her nipples cause such a sweet clench of pleasure deep inside?

She sighed from sheer abandon then gasped as his lips closed over one nipple. It was sensation magnified. Myfanwy closed her eyes and let herself flow in the sheer joy of his lips and the teasing of his tongue. She arched her chest to meet his mouth, letting her head drop back and her breasts curve upward, wordlessly begging for more. He complied. Now her other breast received his kiss, while his nimble fingers caressed the first nipple.

"Arragh," she murmured. He looked up, gold flecks on his wide lips. She touched one fleck and it came off on her fingertip. "That's my gold," she said.

He shook his head. "No, mine. Why do you think they decorated you? Didn't I promise to lick it all off?" Yes. Her throat went dry at the prospect. With a smile, he reached for her finger and slowly licked off the little speck. "I will take off every trace before we fly back across the crater."

She hoped it took years to remove gilding. She wanted his mouth on her again. Immediately!

Never taking his eyes off her face, he climbed onto the divan and stretched beside her. "Not still afraid, are you?" His voice was soft, and as persuasive as his touch on her breast.

"Not of you," she replied.

A crease, almost a frown gathered between his eyes. "What are you afraid of?"

Her jaw clenched with the realization that he expected an answer. Now, as he waited, his hand warm on her breast. It never occurred to her to evade. "Of pain, when you..." She faltered in shame at speaking of these things.

"When I take your maidenhood?" His eyes widened and his voice rose in amazement. She nodded, very much aware of the blush flooding her face. He shook his head and gave her a searching look. "Why would I hurt you?"

Myfanwy swallowed as best she could with a throat tighter than she'd ever thought possible. "They say it is always so. That women must submit and accept."

"They lie!" She jumped at the force in his voice and the near growl that followed. "Myfanwy, my love." His great hand reached out to stroke her face. "I did not mean to frighten you, but they lied." He paused as if to be sure she understood. "I will never give you pain. That I vow before the Goddess. Do you believe me?"

She did believe him, but his words contradicted all she'd ever been taught. "How can it be so?" Her face reddened even more at asking, but how could she reconcile Arragh's promise with all she'd ever been taught?

"How could I hurt you, Myfanwy? You're my mate." He leaned closer and kissed her. "Trust me, when I enter you the first time I'll be small enough to take your maidenhood easily. Later when you're accustomed to me, I'll fill you completely. But I won't be too large at first."

It hardly made sense, but she couldn't disbelieve, or could she? "How is this?" She paused remembering the women's talk. "A man cannot control when he is..." Dear Goddess! What was she saying?

"A man cannot." Arragh smiled. "I'm not a man, Myfanwy."

He wasn't! "I've noticed."

He chuckled. "I should hope so!" He was very close now, hip to hip, leg to leg, and his chest seemed like a great gray wall by her face. "There is no pain between mates who desire each other and you desire me." He paused as his fingers trailed a path between her breasts and down her belly. "I know you do, Myfanwy. I can smell your desire on your body."

Was that what it was? The heated scent between her legs that became noticeable as soon as Arragh spread her open. The hand on her belly eased down, cupping her naked quim and starting wild tremors sparking like fire. Her hips took on a life of their own, shifting and angling upward to feel even more. His response was an increase of pressure until she felt a strong finger rubbing in her slit. Firm, gentle and insistent he stroked in rhythm with her hips.

Her whimpers became moans, her mind became a wild white fog. All her knowing focused on the sweet and soaring pleasure between her legs. "Arragh!" It was almost a mewl, her tongue no longer shaped words.

"Should I stop?" he whispered, his breath warm on her skin.

"No!" Now it was halfway to a scream. What was happening?

"I won't." She heard his promise clearly, understood him for certain but then he moved, shifting away from her.

"Arragh, don't go!" She grasped his shoulder, digging her nails into his dragon skin.

His lips were warm on the back of her hand. "I'm not leaving, my love. I'm about to give you more. Everything you've ever dreamed and some things that never even entered your dreams." He was now seated between her open legs, one hand on the inside of her thigh. His head so low, his breath brushed her bare skin. He looked up from between her legs. "I love the smell of your desire, Myfanwy." His finger slid along her crack, opening her folds, exposing even more of her. She sagged back on the pillows as a slow sigh full of ache and need came from deep in her lungs. Her body waited, hot and heavy, her limbs loose and the space between her legs fiery. Frenzied emotions and longings caught up in her wild longing to have Arragh touch her again. And again. "And I long to taste your sweetness," he murmured just before his tongue swept along her slit.

A great cry of shock, surprise, and wonder burst from her tight chest. She lifted her head to see a wide smile and his dark eyes gleaming at her.

"That pleased you?" he asked, the smugness on his face telling her he already knew.

"Yes!" Speaking got harder by the minute.

"Then lie back." She didn't move, couldn't, while her chest heaved and her heart raced. "Lie down, Myfanwy. If you want more."

For a second, he thought she would refuse, but with a little gasp, she yielded. Her need and arousal beating out her modesty and the twisted fallacies they'd filled her young mind with. She wanted him, that was obvious to the skies. Her deep folds glistened rosy with arousal. She was his for the having and the pleasing. A hand on each thigh opened her wider. He paused just long enough to savor the sweet scent of her sex before skimming her slit with the tip of his tongue. He barely touched her. She no doubt thought he'd stroked with his finger. Fair enough, she would know soon enough the wild joys he had in store for her.

He licked again, keeping his tongue narrow. She gave a contented sigh and her legs relaxed under his hands. Next time, he widened his tongue, applying more pressure as he skimmed again, pausing just as he reached her clit. He watched the quiver of anticipation that reached even her deepest parts, then laid the full flat of his tongue on her warm flesh and licked her from fore to aft then returned without giving her a chance to consider what he'd done. He was rewarded with an unsteady sigh. She'd be moaning, begging, and tossing before he was through.

But he was nowhere near through.

He tasted her again, sweet and needy. Needy for him! His heart seemed to swell at the thought. Myfanwy, daughter of Harwed Rees, lusted for Arragh, the Dragon of Cader Bala. The sight of her—pliant and trusting, spread on the pillows—almost undid him. He fought the urge to take her there and then and claim her as his and the hope of all dragons. He needed to take her gently or risk breaking his promise to never give her pain.

He reined in his desires and concentrated on her satisfaction. Her scent near drove his body wild but he was dragon, not some unfeeling human bent on taking instead of giving. Time for Myfanwy to understand about dragon loving.

He lapped her folds again and was rewarded with a slow, heart-wrung moan. Before her sweet whimpers faded, he bent his head and this time, gently circled her clit with the tip of his tongue. His touch was feather light and smooth but drew a wild response. Her legs shook as tremors worked up her body to her face. She gave a gasp, her chest heaved and wide dark eyes met his.

"Arragh!" she said, her shoulders sagging back on the divan as she caught her breath.

"Yes?" She didn't answer. "Yes, my love?" he repeated.

"What are you doing?" It came out on the tail of a little gasp.

"Want me to stop?" His breathing all but ceased as he awaited her answer.

"Nooooo!" She shook her head. "No, please, don't stop! Please!"

Begging already! He bent his head to hide his smile. Running his fingers along the soft skin on the inside of her thighs, he asked, "You want more?"

Instead of the breathless assent he expected, she gave a little snort and lifted herself up to her forearms until she was half-sitting. "Are you trying to tease me?"

Flushed with desire, she was the most beautiful creature in creation and the pique in her voice only added to her sexiness. "Forgive me, Myfanwy. Permit me to make recompense." Before she could reply to accept or refuse, he dipped his head and tapped her clit with the tip of his tongue. She tensed with pleasure before collapsing back and opening herself even wider as if beseeching his entry.

Soon.

After he'd readied his virgin mate completely.

He lapped at her desire until her moans came in a soft litany of need and her body rippled with her want. As she lay back gasping, Arragh moved her legs one at a time so her feet were flat on the divan. With her knees wide, she was utterly open and available. And his.

His fingers traced the lines of gilding that bordered her slit before spreading her female lips apart. She was flushed with need. The scent of arousal intensified as he held her open. His own need to taste deep grew with his spiraling desire. Curling his tongue, he darted in and out, testing her size and penetrating a little more each time. She was tight and narrow and hot with need. A flicker of his tongue had her squirming. A fingertip on her clit brought out a moan. His breath on her moist flesh wrung sighs from her lips. Soon she'd be his utterly.

Very soon.

He tongued her clit until she couldn't keep still. Her head tossed from side to side, her hips rocked, and her hands clutched at the pillows. Keeping up his rhythm, he penetrated her slowly with just one finger. Feeling the pressure of her maidenhead, he paused momentarily, waiting for her to rock her hips downward. A little extra flutter of his tongue brought the response he needed. As she bore down, he pressed upward.

Her cry of surprise was lost in her groan of passion as he quickened the tempo of his tongue. Never pausing, he drove her passion higher until yelps and wild cries of need echoed off the stone walls. He slid a second finger beside the first. She accommodated him as her muscles tightened around him. He explored her slowly, curling his tongue round her clit while seeking the soft, spongy core of her pleasure with his fingers. A wild cry signaled his success. It was only moments now. His lips, tongue, and fingertips worked in tandem, stretching out her passion, pulling her higher and wilder in her need.

Little mewls and cries became great gasps and moans. She was sweating freely. He intensified his touch. Pushed her harder and higher until her groans became great screams of joy. "Arragh!" she yelled aloud as her climax crashed over her and he slid his fingers deep. Her flesh pulled around him as he touched the neck of her womb. She gave a last shout of triumph and collapsed into a soft, pliant heap of womanhood.

"Arragh," she gasped, reaching out her arms.

He withdrew his fingers and moved up the divan to lie beside her, holding her in his arms as the last ripples of her climax slowed. Limp in his arms, she opened her eyes and looked up at him. And smiled. His dragon soul skittered with possessiveness as he bent over and kissed her on the mouth.

His lips felt cool on her heated skin. Her body still rocked and floated on the wild sensations he'd drawn from her. She was weak and sweaty and worn. Content to lie in Arragh's arms as her mind tried to grasp what had happened. What had happened? Too worn to speak, almost too spent to think, Myfanwy looked up at her dragon lover and smiled.

He smiled back, his eyes glinting dark and a look of smugness and delight on his beautiful face. She wanted to ask him something, but as she tried to remember what it was, he leaned closer and kissed her. Her mouth opened of its own volition, but it was her will that brought her tongue to his, her body that longed for his hands, and her mind that understood the strange sweetness on his lips was her! She was tasting her own essence on her dragon's mouth.

"Arragh," she managed when he at last let her go, "I never dreamed anything could happen like that. It was beyond imagining. Past anything I ever thought possible." She paused for breath. "Will we do it again?"

"Many times." He stroked her forehead and dropped a kiss, his lips cool on her sweaty skin. "But first we have to finish."

There was more! "Finish?" But of course, he had yet to— but how? She bit her lip, he had promised but... "Arragh?"

He kissed her again. Her taste still lingered on his lips. He smoothed her skull with his fingertips. "There is still more joy between us, Myfanwy. Much more."

How could she ever doubt him? She ran her hands over his hard dragon chest, his wide shoulders, and with a courage she only half-understood, down his flat and softer belly, and knew she had to ask. He spoke of mating, but how could they mate as a man and woman might? Where was his cock? Not where a man carried his, that much her eyes and hands knew. She frowned as her fingers paused over a small bulge in his groin. Was this his cock? If so, how?

"What perplexes you, little one?"

She took a deep breath. How did one ask? How could she not? But how to ask? "Arragh, your manly parts?"

"Are readying for you, my love." Even as he spoke, his groin rose. Her jaw dropped as she watched his cock appear, slim and smooth, the skin deep, dark gray but the smooth rounded head was rimmed with gold.

"By the Goddess!" She had to be goggling as well as gaping, but in all the heavens! Never had she seen anything so wondrous. "How do you do that?"

He grinned, a smug male grin that crinkled his eyes and creased his cheeks. "I'm dragon. We can."

Yes, he could. "Just like that?"

He nodded. "Just like that, whenever we want to." He chuckled. "I take it, lady, you're impressed? I salute you."

He did! As he spoke, his gilded cock moved back and forth and then made a small circle in the air.

Maybe laughter wasn't the correct reply. She couldn't help it and even less when he acknowledged her amusement with a sideways bob. "But how? You just make it appear, just like that?"

"Only when I need it." He leaned on his hip so his cock tapped the top of her thigh. "Otherwise I keep it tucked away safely. Like my wings."

"Just like your wings!" She felt like an echo but couldn't take all this in and create independent thoughts at the same time.

"Not exactly." There was that smug grin again. "My wings are always the same size and shape."

"Your cock isn't?"

He tipped her chin so she looked deep into his gleaming eyes. "My cock is whatever I need." He kissed her lightly. "You're a virgin, so I'll be small to enter you easily at first. Then I will grow to fill you completely before we take the ultimate pleasure. Together."

"I want to be filled completely." Was she hearing her thoughts, or had she really spoken that aloud?

"I know," Arragh said, "and I will fill you to the hilt and make our bodies one." Her mouth went dry and her pulse raced at his promise. He moved his hips and his cock rubbed up her leg. "Lie down." His hand pressed her shoulder.

Not yet. First... "Wait, Arragh!" She needed to feel with her hands the cock that would soon be hers. He was warm and smooth and harder than she'd ever imagined flesh could be. As her fingers eased from root to rounded tip, he heated at her touch. "And you become even bigger?" How could he be more marvelous, more beautiful?

"Yes!" He proved his words with action, swelling under her fingers and growing longer by several thumbspans. At her shocked and silent gape, he smiled, running his fingers down the side of her face. "Have no fear, Myfanwy. I will be the perfect size for you." As he spoke, his cock returned to its earlier dimensions. "See? I'm ready, Myfanwy, and so, sweet mate, are you."

She was. Waiting became insupportable. She wanted, needed his cock deep in her—right up to the hilt. She yearned to be taken by the dragon. Nothing in creation mattered more than being his mate, the consort of Arragh of Cader Bala. As his hand reached her neck and slowly caressed her breasts, the tightness in her throat eased, the wildness of her mind calmed, and the present came clearer than ever before. "Yes," she whispered, "I'm ready for you."

His kiss was slow and soft and opened her mouth and her heart as if she'd waited all her life for this one embrace. His touch was on her breast, her head, her neck, her hip, and the soaking heat and need between her legs. As he caressed, he put easy pressure on her hip until she rolled on her side. She balanced on her left hip, Arragh close against her back. His skin rubbed hers, one hand played with her nipple as his knee nudged her right leg forward. She was open and ready. Ready for the warm cock that rubbed her back. Ready for the slow kiss on her shoulder that she felt way deep in her groin. Ready for the teasing play of his fingers on her gilded nipples. Ready for the hard cock that nudged between the crease of her buttocks. Ready for his hand spreading the wetness between her legs. Ready for his fingers opening her. Ready for the trail of kisses beginning on her crown and one by one reaching the nape of her neck. Ready for his cock easing deep inside with infinite and intense purpose.

A great sigh of joy greeted his touch in the very core of her womanhood. Nothing in her life had ever been so right. She was made to mate with Arragh. Made for the wild happiness that flooded her consciousness. Was it possible to taste such joy? Nothing in creation could ever match this!

Until his wonderful dragon cock began to swell, intensifying her joy.

As her breathing quickened, he grew and grew, filling her, pressing the soft sides of her cunt, pushing into her depths, marking her, making her his. There was nothing more she ever wanted, no greater pleasure in the wide world than to lie as one with Arragh.

Until he started to move.

Gradually, easily, he slid out and back. The first few times she barely noticed, but then he quickened his pace, withdrawing a little more each time and reentering with increased force until her body rocked with his. Faster he drove and harder. Her mind shut down. She could no longer think or speak. All she could do was feel his power and let wild little whimpers pass her lips.

His hands grasped her shoulders, holding her down as her soul soared into a great paroxysm of pleasure. Now he was driving into her with a wild heat and power that matched his grunts and her cries. Sweat pooled between her breasts. His damp chest slicked against her back. His legs curled with hers. While his gilded dragon cock exhilarated her soul.

How could one woman feel such joy, such possession, such ecstasy? Her body seemed to soar but this wasn't flying. She'd already flown with Arragh. This was more and everything. This was dragon fucking! A great surge of power flooded deep inside her, drenching her, melding with her own wetness and heat. Her eyes shot open as her senses gathered as if for a leap into creation. She felt white light. Saw her own cries as she climaxed. Smelled Arragh's grunts of satisfaction. And tasted the touch of his skin on hers.

With a soft sigh, she collapsed on the pillows. Arragh's voice came as if through a haze and all the world went pink.

Chapter Seven

Myfanwy awoke, rocking in Arragh's arms as her carried her across the room. She'd fainted. She never fainted! But she'd never made love to a dragon before! She looked up at his beautiful face and smiled. "Mine," he said. The word sounded right into the innermost cockles of her heart.

Nothing in all creation could make her happier.

Arragh held her in his arms as he bathed her. She was more than content to lie back and be washed. She'd been this weak recovering from the fever, but never this contented. No woman in creation had ever been this satisfied.

He dried her with warmed sheets, wrapping her in a fresh dry one before carrying her to a couch near a low table. He fed her sweet fruits and gave her wine from a golden goblet. When she could chew and swallow no more, he held her close as she dozed, replete and contented and content to be possessed.

She woke as the pink light of the setting sun glowed over the horizon of the crater. Arragh was asleep beside her, his leg pinning her to the mattress and his hand on her breast. She propped herself up on an elbow to watch the rise and fall of his great chest and the sweet curve of his mouth as it twitched at one corner. Her body responded, remembering how his mouth worked over her. His fingers shifted a little before relaxing back to cup her breast. Arragh murmured her name in his sleep and her heart raced. Was it possible to die from joy? If so, she was close to expiring. But she wanted to live, to live long with Arragh as her mate, and bear him young fledges so the goodness and wisdom of the dragons would persist and linger on the earth.

To think she'd once believed him a destroyer. How sad that her people had turned from the wisdom of the dragons. If she could only return home and tell the truth. Impossible! She'd be repudiated, declared unclean, if they didn't stone her at first sight or set the flames on her. Myfanwy shuddered, remembering her fear before Arragh swept her in his arms and to safety.

Quiet in her mind, she asked the Goddess to make her fruitful and give peace to Bron and Mary. She felt a pang of sadness that their lives had been stolen by the village they called home.

In the still air, Myfanwy heard the singing, low at first then louder. The dragons were raising another hymn to the heavens! Myfanwy slid out from under Arragh's embrace and walked over to the open doorway and out into the scented garden. Now the volume grew, rich and melodious. She couldn't make out the words, but the joy in the song washed over her in waves of happiness. Without words, she knew the song was for her and Arragh, a celebration of their mating.

"The bed cools without you."

"It was the singing." Her heart tightened as she turned and watched her lover approach. "I came to listen."

He was close now, his arms round her shoulders, enfolding her in the safety of his love. "They're singing about us." His self-satisfied grin told her she'd been right in her guess about the song.

"Oh, yes?"

"Indeed." He pressed closer, her bottom was against his thighs and his hands under her breasts.

"Let's listen." She closed her eyes and leaned into his strength. "What are they singing?" One voice rose clear above the others.

"That's Rarrp." Arragh kissed her on the side of her neck. "She's proclaiming the great power of my cock."

Good heavens! Was she really singing about that? Singing or not, Arragh's cock was growing. She felt his heat and hardness as he pressed against her. One arm now around her waist, his hand covering her belly while his fingertips played her quim. She was wet again. Wanting him. Needing Arragh.

"She's saying you carry my seed inside you and will give birth to a fine young dragon."

"Already?" Was it possible? Yes. But...

"My sister sees what others can't."

"Is she sure?"

"I'm not." He stepped back, tugging at her arm. "But we have days to make certain. Come on." She followed him back under the roof.

"Days?" She wanted to chuckle. His cock looked ready to burst. Hours earlier, his size would have alarmed her. Now it sent her body wet with need.

He clasped her by the waist and held her to him, pressing his cock into the softness of her belly. His eyes glowed blue-green as he looked down at her. "Days, Myfanwy. Whole days and nights." His kiss sent tremors of anticipation across her skin. "And you'll spend them where you belong. In my nest."

Where else?

About the Author

To learn more about Rosemary Laurey, please visit www.rosemarylaurey.com.

Look for these titles by *Rosemary Laurey*

Now Available:

Country Pleasures

Deep Waters

Stone Heart

Heart of the Raven

J. C. Wilder

Dedication

For Audra Hensly—a true lover of fiction and fantasy.

Chapter One

Shivering in her threadbare shift and ragged fur wrap, Dani crouched beside the wheel of her family's wagon. Even with rags wrapped around her feet, her toes were numb. The weak winter sun had faded from the sky several hours earlier, veiling the landscape in icy darkness. She barely acknowledged the discomfort as she'd never known any different. Most of her life had been spent freezing in the winter and burning in the summer.

A few feet away was a small campfire around which crowded her traveling companions. Her father Con was a big brutish man with fists like rocks and a passion for ale. He sat on a tree stump, his clothing rumpled and dirty as he chugged from a jug of cheap Climerian ale.

His younger brother sat next to him. Rayben fancied himself a magician and sorcerer, one the likes of which the world had never seen, or so he said. That part was true at least, as no one had ever seen him actually use magic on anything. From what Dani had witnessed during their long years on the road, his only talent was wenching and swilling ale with her father.

Two recent additions sat huddled around the fire across from her family. The strangers had joined them several days ago, shortly after Dani and her family had been chased from yet another town.

The tall blond one had introduced himself as Dar while the shorter, greasier one was called Knot. Dani wasn't sure if that was really his name or if the deformity on the side of his head caused people to make fun of him to the point that he believed it was his name.

Whatever the reason, Dani knew she wasn't coming out from behind the dubious sanctuary of the wagon wheel until they were long gone. Both men, upon seeing her, had immediately inquired as to the price of her services for a quick fuck. Luckily for her, Con hadn't been that drunk.

Yet.

Having been on the road most of her life, Dani was no innocent. The only reason her father kept her around was because he liked his food prepared for him. Con had sold her older sister, Nova, to another group of travelers like themselves many seasons ago. Her family had been down on their luck yet again and one of the men had offered a handsome sum. Con had turned over his oldest daughter with nary a backward glance.

Dani rubbed her skinny arms and wondered where Nova was now. Was she still alive? The life of a traveler was hard and for a woman ill-used, it was short as well. Living outside under the stars, always stealing the necessities of life and fighting for every mouthful to be had—if Nova had been abandoned, her belly filled with a child... Dani shuddered. It was hard enough to scavenge enough food for one, let alone two, and a woman alone wasn't safe. For most men, it wouldn't matter if she were breeding or not if she was close at hand.

Dani propped her chin on her crossed arms. As long as she remained trapped with her father, she would always be in danger of suffering the same fate as Nova. Realizing this, she'd tried to escape several seasons ago only to be caught by Rayben a few days later. She shifted her foot and the large iron cuff and chain that bound her to the wagon clanked. Her father had stopped in the next town and had the ironsmith imprison his remaining daughter. Con had laughed when she'd told him why she'd run. He told her that Nova was beautiful and men desired her while Dani was as ugly as a boil. No man would ever want to bed her, let alone choose her as a lifemate.

She scowled at her father through the spokes of the wheels. She longed for a place to rest, where people would accept her. A place where she didn't have to fight for every morsel of food and a place to lay her head. To have someone to love her for who she was and, most of all, to make her own decisions about where she went and what she did. That was Dani's idea of real freedom.

Not everyone in the world traveled. There were quite a few settlements in the southlands where people lived and worked together to keep home and hearth intact. An overseer governed those privileged enough to live in such a settlement and those families didn't have to move like the travelers. They lived in cities surrounded by peaceful farmland. Even the poorest family had a small home, a plot of land, farm animals and enough food to eat. They didn't sleep in the mud and run from town to town one step ahead of the peacekeepers.

She'd been to one of those cities once. All had been welcome in Malian, even the travelers, as long as they abided by the rules of the overseer. The only time in her life she'd slept with a roof over her head was within the confines of that city. But that had been many years ago, before her mother had died when Dani was but a child.

After her mother's death, Con had gotten them kicked out of Malian. He, Rayben and Jod, the eldest brother who now languished in a Sladerian prison for murder, had been caught stealing horses from the overseer.

As long as Dani lived, she would never forget the night she'd been rousted from her warm bed and summarily tossed into the streets. Warriors of the overseer had towered over her, their gray uniforms emblazoned with the Malian emblem had made them look ten feet tall, as the impatient hooves of the horses had ground their meager possessions into the mud. Never would she forget how the mighty Malian warriors had looked at her as if she were trash—something distasteful to be swept forever out of sight. She and her family had been escorted to the city limits and forbidden to return.

Dani shuddered and drew her arms tighter around her knees. Even now, so many years later, she still suffered from occasional nightmares of that horrific night.

Ever since then, they'd traveled from town to town, her father gambling and stealing what he could while Rayben concocted potions to cure ailments and performed slight of hand tricks that resulted in liberated gold coins from his victims. Her job was to cook the stolen food and forage when it was necessary. Lately it had been necessary more than not.

"Girl! Where are you, you lazy whore?"

Dani jumped at her father's strident tone. He never called her by name. It was always "girl". Sometimes she wondered if he even remembered her name or that she was his flesh and blood.

She rose to her feet and shuffled around the wagon. The thick iron cuff on her ankle made walking slow. She'd padded the inside of the cuff with dried grasses to keep the chafing to a minimum, but the miniscule layer did little to save her skin from abuse.

"Yes?"

"'Bout time, you lazy wench." Con scooped up the dice and dropped them into a leather cup, jiggling it before tossing the dice into the dirt again. "Bring me another jug and be quick about it."

Dani reached into the wagon and pushed the heap of smelly blankets aside. As soon as the weather warmed, she'd have to wash the blankets and clothes. Until then they'd just have to stay dirty. It's not as if the men ever noticed anyway. She located a pottery flask of ale in the back of the wagon. With short mincing steps, she walked to her father, doing her best to avoid Knot and Dar.

"'Bout time." He snatched the flask from her grip. "You're as slow as a Sladerian sloth and twice as ugly. Get out of my sight," he snarled. "I don't want to see your face before morn. Do ye hear, girl?"

Dani scrambled back toward the wagon, the chain hampering her, and she received a sharp pinch on her buttock that sent her stumbling. She shot Knot an evil glare as she made her way back to the wagon. Grabbing her meager bedroll from the back, she slipped under the wagon into the dubious safety offered between its wheels.

She unfolded a small grass mat and placed it on the cold, hard ground. Sitting up with her back against the wheel, she tucked her knees tightly to her chest as she wrapped a shabby blanket around herself. The blanket was too small and threadbare to do much but every little bit helped.

Weary, she leaned her head back and closed her eyes. The noise of the men around the fire slurping ale and expelling noxious gases from their back ends faded as another scene, a favored scene, took shape in her mind's eye.

She sat at a massive dining table laden with every type of food imaginable. Stuffed pheasant, smoked fish, and freshly roasted fowl resided in massive troughs. Bowls of spring greens cooked with pork and onion sat next to a towering arrangement of fresh fruits. Her mouth watered and her stomach rumbled. She was *so* hungry it was all she could do to not throw herself face first into the feast.

Dani reached out for a hunk of steaming hot bread and caught sight of her arm. Encrusted dirt turned her pale skin to a dark brown. Ashamed of her dirty clothes and body, she pulled her arm back as a hooded servant approached.

"No, miss. You cannot have any food until you submit."

She cocked her head. "Submit to what?"

"To him." He gestured behind her. "Submit to him and your heart will be full as well as your belly."

Dani turned to see a massive raven perched on a windowsill. Its intelligent black eyes regarded her for a moment, then its beak parted with a wild screech. She shivered, afraid yet curious at this new development. Why would the servant want her to submit to a bird?

As if the creature could read her thoughts, the raven flicked out its wings and beat them, creating small torrents of air that caressed her skin. As she watched, the tempo increased until the torrents pulled at her clothing and the earth trembled.

Startled, Dani jerked awake to realize that the earth was indeed trembling. Near the fire, Con and Rayben lurched to their feet as two men entered the clearing astride their towering horses. For a second, she thought the peacekeepers from the last village had caught up with them. But neither the men nor the horses bore the all too familiar bronze shield worn by the peacekeepers.

The black stallions were at least seventeen hands tall, towering well over her family. Rayben backed away from the first horse, his fists wrapped around the handle of his sword he held before him. The firelight illuminated the poorly maintained blade.

"Greetings, travelers." The blond man nearest the fire slid off his horse. He was dressed from head to toe in black. His knee-boots were polished to a high sheen and his tightly fitted pants were tailored to muscular thighs. His broad chest and shoulders were clad in black leather. Every inch of him proclaimed wealth.

"May we share your fire for a spell?" His voice was cultured and carried none of the northland accent that she'd expected. With his lilting tones, he was definitely from the southland.

Con gave Rayben a nod. Of course they'd allow the newcomers to join them as they were both richly garbed. No doubt her family planned to get them drunk and take them for all they were worth. Con would get them drunk and Rayben would swap the dice for a loaded set that would play in their favor. It was an old ploy, one that had been performed many times before.

Dani settled back against the wheel as the second newcomer left his horse. He too was clad in black, but he wore a full cloak and hood. In the glow of the fire she caught only a brief glimpse of his strong jaw. He was several inches taller than the blond man but moved with the same loose-limbed grace.

She shivered and wondered if his cloak were warm. Maybe Con would give her the cloak after they'd stolen everything else the men had to offer. She caught sight of Con eyeing the cloak as the men introduced themselves. Then again, maybe not.

He had to be a very rich man to afford such a garment. Black wool lined with matching black fur. For a moment, Dani wished she could surround herself in the silky fur instead of her smelly scratchy blanket.

Her eyes closed and she fell into a light doze. Dreams of warm fur and mountains of food tormented her. As the night wore on, sounds from the group around the fire were woven into her dreams. From time to time, she opened her eyes, seeing them play dice as they imbibed. She watched as the cloaked one raised the bottle to his lips. He really had a nice mouth, well-shaped lips. He lowered the bottle and licked the remaining droplets of wine from them. She wondered what it would feel like to have a man lick wine from her skin.

A shout roused her from a deep sleep. She stirred, peering out at the sky through the spokes of the wheel. It was full dark, sunrise still hours away. The temperature had dropped and frost had formed on the grass. It was both beautiful and deadly.

"You imbecile!"

Dani looked over to see her father raging at Rayben.

"What were you thinking? You just lost everything," he shouted. Dar and Knot sat together, shooting worried glances at the newcomers to Con and back again.

The two men in black sat on the far side. The one with the cloak sat silent and still, the hood still shielding his face. The other had an amused expression though his dark eyes were alert, waiting, measuring. She had the feeling he missed very little. Whatever had happened while she'd slept, it didn't seem to be good.

"I lost it all..." Rayben whispered.

"Damn right you did," Con shouted. "You've ruined us."

"And you still owe them." Knot nodded at the two men. "You can't even fulfill your last bet."

Dani bit her lip. It would appear for the first time her father had failed in his plans. Instead of stealing from the newcomers, he himself had been fleeced. She couldn't prevent a small smile which she quickly hid behind her hand.

"Indeed?" The blond with the shiny boots spoke. "You cannot pay the two thousand credits owed?"

Her eyes widened. Two thousand credits was a princely sum, one she'd never seen in her life. How could her uncle have done this? What would have possessed him to make such a wager?

"Surely we can come to some arrangement—" Con began.

The man shook his blond head. "'Tis the credits or your life." He shrugged, but Dani didn't miss the glitter in his eyes. Her heart sped as she leaned forward.

"I have one possession worth what you ask." Con licked his lips. "If you'll allow me to retrieve it."

The blond glanced at the hooded man who gave a slow nod. A trickle of unease ran down her back as Con lumbered to his feet. What could he have that was worth such a sum? Dani was familiar with every possession packed in the spindly wagon and knew there was nothing of such value.

"Where are you, girl?" he hissed.

Dani released her grip on the ragged blanket and started to scoot out from underneath the wagon.

"What—"

A strong, fleshy hand wrapped around her ankle and yanked her from her secluded hideout. She grunted as her shift slid up and the rocks and coarse grass dug into the skin of her buttocks and thighs. She grabbed the hem and tugged it down as Con hauled her to her feet.

"I need you."

"For what?"

"Hush." He turned and dragged her toward the fire.

Eyes down, she stumbled in his bruising grip, her heart in her throat.

"My slave." Con shoved her onto her knees directly across from the men in black. "She's worth far more than the debt at stake and she's mine to do with what I will."

Dani's head came up. Did her father just offer her to cover his debts? While her flesh and blood had been nothing but a burden to her, she'd never dreamed he'd sell her to the highest bidder as he had Nova. Her sister had been beautiful while she was...just Dani. No man would want her.

Through the flickering flames, the blond stared at her, a revolted expression on his face. Whether it was she or the recent turn in events that repulsed him she didn't know, but she shook Con's proprietary hand off her shoulder and straightened her spine. Damned if she would cower beneath the gaze of the strangers.

"Hey now," Knot objected. "She's a fresh piece and I want first dibs on her."

Dani cringed as his stubby fingers landed on her arm, squeezing her flesh. The stench of cheap ale and rancid tobacco assailed her. She'd die before she would submit to any man, especially Knot.

"Doesn't appear she's thrilled with that idea," the blond man drawled.

Con reached over and removed Knot's hand. "She's payment for my debt. Unless you can produce two thousand credits, keep your hands to yourself."

"One roll for the whole wager," the blond said to Knot.

Knot looked at her and licked his lips. "One roll, for everything?"

The blond nodded and his partner remained silent.

"Even the girl?" Dar asked.

"She's part of the prize, is she not?" The blond shrugged.

"Aye—"

"Nay," Dani cried out.

"Hush."

Con swiped at her but she moved too slowly. His knuckles caught her lip and she tasted blood. She fell sideways and tried to scramble away on her hands and knees. Someone grabbed the chain around her ankle and yanked, sending her face down on the ground. Raucous laughter erupted as her tormentor hauled on the chain, pulling her back toward the fire.

Her nails dug into the cold earth as she tried to prevent her return. Her shift caught on the grass, and before she could stop it, her backside was exposed to the cold night air.

"Now there's a sight," Dar roared.

"Aye, and I think I'll take a taste now." Knot's voice sounded over her head. The flat of a hand smacked against her backside, then gave her a squeeze, eliciting a shriek from her.

Humiliated, Dani struggled to get away as tears stung her eyes.

"Leave her." The quiet command brought the other men to a standstill.

Taking advantage of her freedom, Dani scrambled as far as the chain would allow. She drew her knees up and pulled down the shift to cover as much of her body as possible. Her buttocks ached where Knot had hit her and her pride stung even more.

Across the fire, the hooded one stood in the shadows. No doubt he was the one who'd spoken.

"Finish the game," he spoke to his companion. "Then let's be on our way. We have far to journey before daylight breaks."

Rayben reached for the leather cup and the scattered dice. After collecting them, he shook the cup before he spilled the dice into the packed dirt.

Against her will, Dani scrambled to her knees, eyes straining to see the marks on the squares of carved bone.

Seven.

She shot a look at her father's stoic face where he stood over his brother's shoulder. She knew he didn't care one whit what happened to her, but he'd care the moment he had to prepare his own meals. By then it would be too late.

Rayben gathered the dice with a shaky hand before he passed them to Knot. Dar snatched the cup away from Knot, then quickly shook and tossed them onto the ground.

Fifteen.

Knot gave a delighted chuckle, then blew her a kiss as he rubbed his crotch. Her stomach rolled and she averted her gaze.

The blond man leaned forward, the firelight streaking his shiny hair with gold. With an easy grace he scooped the dice into the cup and shook it. He glanced over his shoulder at his silent companion before he tossed the dice with a flourish.

Dani rose to her feet, leaning forward to peer over the fire and behold her fate.

Seventeen.

They'd won. Stunned, she looked at the blond man then the hooded figure. A shiver ran down her back at the thought of being at the mercy of these two.

"I want the girl." Dar rose from the ground and adjusted his belt over his substantial belly. "How much for her?"

The blond looked at her then at his silent friend and, though not a word was spoken, some sort of silent communication passed between the men. The blond nodded. "Girl, what's your name?" he asked.

She clutched her ragged dress to her chest, desperate to retain even the slightest shred of dignity. "Dani. My name is Dani."

"Well, Dani, what would you like to do? Stay here with these men?" He waved his hand to indicate her family and the recent additions. "Or travel south a piece with us?"

She glanced at her stoic father. If she remained with him, he would no doubt sell her again, possibly even to Knot and Dar who'd use her as a whore. Of that there was no doubt in her mind.

She looked at the blond and his silent friend. She didn't know what they offered for the future. Would they kill her and leave her body by the road? Would they sell her again? Whatever the outcome, the choice was hers. For the first time in her life, Dani felt the heady anticipation of the unknown.

Mustering her courage, she nodded. "I'll go with you. I should like to travel south."

The hooded one turned away toward his horse as if her answer were of no concern. The blond rose from his seat on the ground and stretched his long body. "Prepare yourself as we'll leave shortly." He, too, turned to attend his horse.

Dani scrambled for the wagon, eager to grab her meager possessions and escape. The chain hampered her gait, but she managed to grab her tattered mat, blanket and the small wooden box that contained all she owned in the world.

"Remove the chain from her leg," the hooded one spoke.

Con crossed his arms over his chest, a smirk on his face. "I no longer have the key."

The hooded one glanced at his companion before he slid off his horse. His fur-lined cape flared as he walked toward Dani. She tightened her grip around the box as fear ignited in her belly.

I will show no fear...I will show no fear...

As he passed Knot, his elbow shot out and he knocked the drunken sot onto his backside with barely a movement. He withdrew a long gleaming sword.

Would he kill her rather than take her along?

I will show no fear...I will show no fear...

Dani squared her shoulders. She'd be damned before she'd show fear to this creature. Kill her or not, she'd not quiver before him.

He paused ever so slightly and she had the feeling he was assessing her. For a moment, they stood facing each other, each measuring the other's worth. He shoved the hood from his face and she was struck by the sheer magnetism he possessed. Shadowed eyes regarded her from beneath his dark brows. Carved masculine cheekbones and a sharp nose gave him an intelligent look, but his mouth gave him away. Thin lipped, the bottom slightly fuller than the top, they twitched as if he were trying hard not to smile.

Dani felt that he must have approved of her as he didn't remove her head from her shoulders. With a swift downward stroke he severed the chain that bound her to the wagon and her miserable life. He returned to his horse, not waiting for her to follow.

"You'll ride with me, little one." The blond held out his hand and slid his foot from the stirrup so she might use it.

Dani eyed the massive horse with misgiving. She'd never ridden a horse before, but she'd bite off her tongue before she'd admit it. Before she could move, hands grasped her hips and lifted her high onto the horse. She clutched her belongings as she tried to find her seat.

"Grip with your knees and put your stuff in front of you." The cloaked one spoke in her ear, his big hands spanning her waist.

Hands trembling, Dani laid the mat and blanket across her lap and tucked the chest into her belly. Just as her hands latched onto the blond's waist, he wheeled the horse and they moved into the woods. She couldn't resist looking over her shoulder one last time.

Her father was staring into the darkness away from her. Rayben stood beside him, staring into the fire. Knot was rising from the ground, a murderous expression on his face as he glared at the hooded one who was mounting his horse. Dar picked up the jug of ale and hefted it in her direction as if to salute her on her way.

She turned away and fixed her gaze on the stars over the blond's right shoulder. Never again would she allow herself to look back when there was a new life before her.

Chapter Two

"She smells."

Haaken glanced at his brother before his gaze stole to the pathetic creature seated behind Ty on the horse. The slave huddled against his broad back, her dirty fingers clutching his waist. She'd pulled a ragged blanket to shelter her head and shoulders from the cold air. Beneath the hem of her tattered shift dirty legs stuck out, her feet bound in filthy rags.

"We'll seek shelter ahead." Haaken nudged his horse ahead of his younger brother, knowing it would irritate him to no end.

The path through the dark woods narrowed and Haaken rode easily, yet alert with his hand resting on the hilt of his sword. They were within a day of home, but one could never be too careful as these were dangerous times.

He frowned at the thought of the woman behind Ty. Why had he opted to take her with them? The last thing they needed was to add another problem to slow them down even further. It was bad enough the entire trip had been wasted and now they were late on top of it. They'd been due in Wryven two days ago and had no time to dawdle.

After another hour of hard riding, the road widened and he saw a familiar low squat building crouched on the very edge of the lane. Golden light spilled from a lone window, illuminating the way.

"We'll rest here," Haaken said. As he reined in his horse, he heard his brother mutter something, but he ignored him. Normally they wouldn't have stopped at all, preferring to push onward. But with the unexpected addition of the girl, they would be better served to take their rest.

He climbed from his mount in time to see her slide off the horse and fall to the ground. Her expression was half-hidden under lank dirty hair. Clutching her small box and ragged blanket, she glared at Ty.

Now that he was standing downwind of her, he agreed the woman was definitely dirty. He couldn't tell for sure, but he'd bet that her hair was light, possibly blonde. Underfed, dirty and with a perpetual scowl on her face, they'd certainly acquired a winner this time.

He dropped the reins, knowing that Nefri was well trained and wouldn't stray more than a few feet. The sky was lightening and the sun would breach the sky within minutes. They had to hurry.

"Bring her." Ignoring Ty's dismayed expression, Haaken grabbed the woman's arm and hauled her upright. He could feel her shivering through his leather gloves. Once she was steady, he released her and strode to the door of the inn. Ty would have to see to the horses and the woman as he wouldn't have time.

The door opened easily and the smell of overcooked meat and spilled ale assaulted him as he stepped into the overly warm interior. The taproom was large, taking up nearly the entire first floor of the building. At each end of the room was a large fireplace with long tables scattered between. Along the far wall was the bar and a gnome-like man was wiping down the battle-scarred top. Judging from the dingy gray color of the cloth, Haaken doubted he was doing more than stirring the grime from one spot to another.

"We're closed," he barked without looking up.

Haaken ignored him and walked closer. He opened the small pouch tied to his sword belt and withdrew three gold coins, more money than this establishment would bring in during a fortnight.

"Get the hell out of here. I said we're—" The bartender looked up and his eyes widened. "S-s-sire." He dropped the cloth he'd been pushing. "I didn't realize—"

"Private rooms." He tossed the first coin on the bar, watching as the man grabbed and then bit it to ensure its authenticity. "Food." He tossed the second coin, which the bartender caught with a gasp. "A bath and change of clothing for one of my companions." He held up the third coin so the little man could see it but not reach for it. "If everything is to my satisfaction, this too will be yours." He tucked it back into his waist pouch for safekeeping.

"Yes, sire. Right away." The bartender's gaze was locked on Haaken's money pouch. He licked his lips then nodded, eager to do as he was bid. "Do you desire your usual rooms?" He walked out from behind the bar, wiping his dirty hands on an equally filthy apron. "We're empty this eve, business has been slow."

"Be quick about it, we're tired."

"Of course, sire." The man offered a sketchy bow.

Behind him, the inn door opened for Ty and the girl. His brother was behind her, trying to push and it was obvious she didn't want to enter. Her feet were stuck straight out in front of her and one hand clutched the frame. Ty tried to unhook her hand from the door then howled when she twisted and bit him.

"Yowww!" He grabbed her by the waist and swung her around so hard she was forced to grab her box with both hands or risk dropping it. He dumped her on the floor, then slammed the door shut behind him, preventing her escape.

"What's going on out here?" A large woman entered the room, the top of her dress undone though she seemed in no hurry to cover her enormous breasts. Her eyes widened as she caught sight of the woman on the floor. "You can't bring *that* in here."

As she marched toward Ty and the woman, another man stomped out of the room she'd just vacated. "Woman, get back here! I paid for a fuck and—" With his drawers drooping from his skinny ass, the man took one look at Haaken and made an awkward run for the door.

"Wife!" The bartender moved to head her off.

Clearly the innkeeper had married since their last visit. Haaken glanced from the diminutive bartender to his new wife. Judging from the disparity in their sizes, he was surprised the man hadn't smothered under all that flesh.

"I run a clean place," she screeched at her husband.

Haaken glanced at the disarray of the room, toppled tankards and grease-spotted tabletops. If she ran a clean place, she certainly didn't mean this one.

He stepped forward. "Mistress, I can assure you that you'll be well compensated for your aid."

The bartender's wife stopped in mid-screech when she saw him. Her skin flushed and her gaze moved over him as if he were a plate of candied fruit and she were a starving woman.

"Well." She shook off her husband's arm and approached Haaken with a sway in her step. "Since you put it so nicely." She gave him a heated smile with dingy teeth as he caught the aroma of unwashed flesh, sweat and another man's satisfaction.

He moved away from the woman. "As I said, you'll be well compensated. My brother will stable the horses while you'll aid the young woman in getting cleaned up and properly clothed."

109

"I don't have anything that'll fit such a scrawny creature," the woman sneered.

"Anything will do as long as she's covered and clean."

The bartender picked up the two bundles Ty had brought in. "Who is she, milord?"

"Your whore?" the wife asked.

Haaken's gaze flicked over the girl still seated on the floor. Dani? Was that her name? In her current state, it would take more of a man than he to bed the repulsive creature. Her smell alone would keep most men at a distance. "My slave." He turned and walked toward the doorway leading to the steps and the rooms above.

"I'm no man's slave," the young woman spoke. Haaken turned to see her struggle to her feet. She limped into the center of the room, her chin high and the tail of her chain clanking on the floor. "I wasn't Con's slave nor will I ever be yours." Her stormy blue eyes sparked with indignation. Even though she swayed with weariness and was coated in layers of dirt, he was pleased to see that she had some spark of life left in her.

He glanced down at the rusted iron cuff that encircled her ankle for it told another story. Freewomen weren't bound like dogs to rickety old wagons. "See to it the cuff is removed as well." He continued up the stairs.

The Boar and the Ram was a familiar tavern. Several times a year, he and his men visited the establishment and he knew the layout well. He walked to the broad door at the end of the hall and flung it open. The room was small, but clean and well ordered. A large bed, washstand, a window overlooking the lane and a fireplace with a comfortable chair were all it boasted.

The bartender entered with an armload of wood. He dumped it into the wood box, then crouched to light the fire already laid. Two sleepy-eyed maids appeared, one with a fresh pitcher of water and the other with a tray of wine, sliced meat and crusty bread.

As they moved about making the room comfortable, Haaken removed his cape and draped it over the foot of the bed. They had no idea he was going to have little use for the room.

After a few moments and a number of curtseys and bows, they left and Haaken bolted the door behind them. Picking up the tray of food, he opened the narrow door in the far corner. It opened with very little sound and he stepped into the confining space.

His eyes quickly adjusted to the darkness and he climbed the spiral steps to an attic. On the east side of the cavernous space was a large dormer window with an old velvet chair and small table positioned before it. Haaken put the tray on the table and opened the window, allowing the cool air to rush into the musty space. Seating himself in the comfortable expanse of the chair, he finally allowed his body to relax.

The sun continued its inexorable climb while he cleaned the tray and drank the wine. As the sun broached the horizon and he closed his eyes, he heard the first scream.

They were going to kill her.

Heart pounding, Dani slid from under the arm imprisoning her. Her feet skidded across the damp stone floor as she scrambled under a rickety table in the corner of the room. She pressed her back against the wall and her fingers curled around the wooden legs as curses from the fat woman rang overhead.

That horrible blond man had taken her chest away from her and shoved her into this place. Even though he'd told her she'd get it back, she didn't believe him. He probably wanted to steal all of her treasures and now that he had them, they wanted her dead.

No way would she make it easy on these demons.

"No amount of money in the world is worth this ruckus, not even for the handsome Lord-Whoever-He-Is. Unless of course he gives me a good screw before he fucks this one." The fat woman brayed then dropped to her knees, her eyes glittering with devilish intent. "Come out here, you dirty wench."

Dani kicked at the large coarse hands reaching for her. Fingers dug into her ankle and the large woman gave a sharp tug that slid Dani across the floor. Still clinging to the table legs, the length of her arms stopped her forward progress.

"Loosen her grip," the woman snapped at a nearby maid.

The little maid clawed at Dani's fingers and still she refused to release the splintery wood. If she lost her hold, they'd kill her for sure. The maid slapped at her hand and Dani felt a brief moment of triumph until she felt teeth sink into her knuckles.

"Yeow!" She released her fingers and the fat woman gave a vicious yank, propelling her across the damp floor. Dani rolled to her stomach and kicked at the woman's hands, desperate to free herself.

"Red!" her tormentor screamed. "Get in here."

The door flew open and a massive man filled the doorway, his hair as red as the setting sun. For a split second, Dani froze. What new demon was about to be let loose upon her?

The grip on her ankles loosened and Dani took the opportunity to give another kick, managing to free herself. The fat woman lunged again and Dani gave another kick, unbalancing her and she stumbled back against the wall.

"Get her," the woman snarled. "Put her into the tub."

A big hand landed on the back of Dani's neck, halting her awkward scramble for safety. Nails dug into her skin as she was hauled to her feet and steered toward a steaming tub of water.

She struggled against the restraining grip, but this was no overfed woman. This was a full-grown man who was built as if he were no stranger to wielding a sword all day, every day.

She gave a startled shriek as the giant pushed her into the narrow metal tub. The scalding water soaked her meager clothes and seared her skin. Ruthlessly, her head was shoved under the water and she struggled against the punishing hands as water filled her mouth and nose.

Fingers tangled in her hair and hauled her head above the water. She gasped for air as she struggled to raise her leg over the side of the tub. Her ankle, the one that had been tortured by the iron cuff, was abraded and the scorching water sent such pains up her leg that her teeth hurt.

"Stop fighting," the giant rumbled.

"I'm not—" Her words were cut off as he shoved her back under the water. She struggled, her lungs unprepared and straining against the lack of oxygen. It hurt, it hurt so bad and she wasn't sure she could stand it much longer.

Then she was hauled to the surface again and she coughed water from her lungs as she hung her head over the edge, struggling to breathe.

"Are you through?" the giant asked.

Weak, she nodded and tried to raise her leg from the hot water.

"Why are you trying to get out?" he rumbled.

She shrieked as she was shoved under the water again, this time only for a split second before she was hauled to the surface again. The pain from her abused scalp brought tears to her eyes as he dunked her again, too fast to catch her breath. Was he going to kill her?

"Hurt." She gasped as he pulled her up again.

He paused, his fingers still tangled in her hair. "What hurts?"

"Ankle...hurts." Her lower lip began to tremble. "Please..."

The giant released her and, with curiously gentle fingers, he captured her leg and raised it to rest on the edge of the tub. She winced as his finger found a sore and she heard his sharp intake of breath.

He patted her knee, his touch tender. "I'll get something so I can remove this right away."

Shocked at his sudden change, it was all Dani could do to simply nod. He released her leg and strode from the room, careful to shut the door behind him.

"Remove her clothes," the fat woman ordered the little maid.

Dani began shrugging out of her clothes when the maid stepped forward. After her clothes were removed, she saw the fat woman coming at her with a large bristle bush and a bar of soap. Did she actually think to *wash* her with that? Where was the bathing cloth?

Dani cleared her throat, her voice husky from her dunking. "If you have a cloth I can—"

"Shut up. I won't take any more of your bad behavior. His lordship bade me to get you clean and that's what I mean to do."

The maid returned armed with another brush and soap as well. Within seconds, they held her down and were scrubbing her skin as if she were a soiled garment. Dani shrieked and fought to avoid the torturous bristles to no avail. One of them had her hair in a firm grip as they sought to flay the skin from her very bones.

Reality receded to a red haze of too-hot water, sharp bristle brushes and harsh ash soap as the two women scrubbed her within an inch of her life. She didn't even flinch when the maid announced her hair beyond saving. With a sharp knife, they cut off most of it in knotted, uneven hunks.

When they were done, the maid ushered Dani from the black water and into a thin towel, tossing a second one over her ruined hair.

"Ye Gods, woman, he bade you to bathe her, not skin her alive."

Dani didn't move as Red's voice boomed across the room.

"She was fighting us," the fat woman said. "She got what she asked for." She walked around the red-haired giant and slammed the door behind her.

Liar.

But Dani was too miserable to utter the word aloud. Every inch of her body ached and her head throbbed from the repeated dunking and rough haircut. Hunched over, she clutched the thin cloth to her body and shivered.

"Go ready her room." Red approached, his work-scarred boots moving into her line of vision.

Dani heard the maid scurry from the room but she refused to look up, not wishing to see what new hell was about to be launched upon her. She started as something touched her shoulders and a length of pale yellow cloth was draped over her. The material was soft as silk yet thick. She shivered and gathered it around her, grateful for its warmth.

Without saying a word, Red dropped to his knee and lifted the foot with the cuff. Withdrawing a long narrow tool, he set to work on the locking mechanism and, within seconds, the old cuff opened enough for him to slide her foot free. The skin abused by the cuff was red and scored from the constant friction.

He looked up at her and his expression was kind. "You're free."

"If only that were true," she said before thinking.

His gaze sharpened. "Lord Haaken is a good man and he'll take fine care of you." He dropped the cuff and released her leg. "Come, I'll take you to your room."

Dani struggled to her feet, careful to avoid his helping hand. Silent, she followed him into the chilly hall and up a narrow set of steps. He opened a door, then stepped aside, allowing her to precede him.

The room was small and a fire crackled in the fireplace. A young woman, not the one who had tortured her, was turning back the bed. Small and narrow but plumped high with soft-looking sheets and blankets, the bed was the best-looking thing Dani had ever seen.

"Good night, miss."

Before she could utter a word, Red shut the door and left the two women alone.

"I have a gown for you, miss."

Dani reluctantly released her yellow wrap and allowed the woman to help her into the thin gown. Within moments, she was tucked into bed in a voluminous white garment. The maid doused the light and slipped from the room, leaving Dani alone with the crackling fire.

Exhausted, she could barely keep her eyes open let alone find the energy to enjoy the unknown luxury of her rented bed. So much had happened in the past few hours. After years of dreaming of freedom, she'd finally escaped her father, not as a free woman, but as a slave to a stranger. What would he do with her? What would become of her? Red had said that her keeper was a good man. She could only hope and pray to Ola that he was right.

Her eyes closed as she allowed her body to sink into the soft mattress. Until she could gain her freedom, as long as her keeper provided clean sheets and a warm bed, she would do almost anything he required of her.

Chapter Three

Haaken scowled at the shorn creature seated at the table in the corner of the private dining room. His little slave had lost not only her dirt and stench, she'd lost yards of hair as well. Her unevenly cut, fuzzy blonde hair stuck up in tufts that made her look like a baby chick. She'd been shorn then sent to bed with wet hair.

Other than her unfortunate haircut, he could see the potential she held. Her eyes were pale blue, surrounded by long blonde lashes. Her features were sharp, too sharp from lack of proper nutrition. Her mouth was soft and full, but her lips were chapped from the cold weather. Ren would have something to aid their healing.

With her gaze locked on her overloaded plate and her feet tucked under voluminous skirts, she stuffed food into her mouth as quickly as she could chew. Ty sat across from her, his food untouched, a look of horrified fascination on his face as she plowed her way through a platter of roasted fowl, fresh cheese and boiled greens.

If she kept eating like this, she'd make herself sick. There was no doubt that she needed the nourishment. Another twenty to thirty pounds would easily sit on her medium-sized frame. Just not all at once.

"Are we ready to leave?" Haaken asked.

She jumped when he spoke; her gaze darting in his direction, then away again. He was mildly irritated that she didn't immediately respond to his question. Obviously her former master had been lax with her training, something he would soon rectify.

Ty pushed away his plate and tossed her an amused look. "After she's done stuffing herself like a fat little sow, we can leave."

She ignored Ty, her cheeks plumped with food like a little yellow nuthatch storing food for a long, hard winter. She snagged a large hunk of brown bread from a plate. Her oversized sleeve slid along her arm and Haaken caught sight of several long red scratches against her pale skin before she stashed the bread in the folds of her skirt.

Before he could think, his hand locked around her wrist as she reached to swipe another piece of the coarse bread.

She gave a squeak of alarm as he pulled her arm up and her sleeve fell away. The long scratches were intersected with smaller ones, especially along the inside of her arm. He turned her arm first this way, then that as he inspected her. The marks were fresh and the echo of terrified screams reverberated through his head.

"When did this happen?" His tone came out harsher than he'd intended and her eyes widened, her mouth still full. "Swallow."

It took her several seconds and she had to reach for a pewter goblet of water to ease the way. His impatience increasing with every second, he resisted the urge to tap his foot.

"Last night." She wiped her mouth with the back of her hand.

"The innkeeper's wife did this to you?" He turned her hand over and noted the teeth marks on her knuckles. "She *bit* you as well?"

She shook her head and the little blonde tufts wobbled. "It was the maid that bit me—"

Haaken hauled her from the chair and pulled her toward the door. The sound of her stolen food falling from her skirt marked their way across the room.

"Gather our things. We're leaving." He spoke to Ty as they exited the room.

The journey to the taproom was short. With her slender wrist still in his grasp, she stumbled along behind him. Her fingers latched onto his cape as she struggled to keep up with him.

The public taproom was packed with customers. The moment Haaken entered, a hush fell over the crowd, punctuated by shushing sounds for those slow to notice his entrance. The bartender looked up from drawing a pint that he handed off before hurrying toward them.

"I trust all is well, sire—"

"No, it is not. Where is your *wife*?"

"My wife, sire?" The bartender began a jittering backward walk. "I'll—"

"I'm here." The overfed woman stepped out from a curtained alcove, adjusting her massive breasts within the sheer confines of her top. She ran her hand over her tousled hair and gave Haaken a come hither look.

"I asked you to assist my companion in a bath." Haaken pulled his reluctant slave in front of him. "Not skin her alive." He held out her arm for both the bartender and his wife to see the marks. Several of the more adventurous customers leaned forward to get a good look at the spectacle.

"She was fighting us and got knocked around a bit." The woman shrugged. "We had to use scrub brushes on her as she was filthy. A simple cloth would never have gotten her clean."

"No one is filthy enough to require their skin to be flayed from their bodies." Haaken pulled the gold coin from his belt pouch. "This was to be payment for the bath and her clothing. As you've seen fit to cause my charge great pain and suffering, I'll award the coin to her for her trouble instead."

"Now, you wait just a—"

"Merlee—" The bartender plucked at her sleeve.

She shook him off and stepped closer to Haaken. "I did as you asked."

"Mistress, you forget yourself." Ty appeared with their saddlebags. "You're speaking to an Overseer appointed by the Realm and you will give him the respect that is his due. Your behavior is not only offensive, but inappropriate. If you wish to remain in our good graces, I recommend you shut up and take your loss with good grace."

Haaken released Dani and flipped her the coin. Several people exclaimed as light flashed over the rich gold before she snatched it in mid-air and tucked it into a fold in her clothes. He retrieved his bag from Ty and turned to leave, his anger appeased.

For now.

Dani clutched Ty's waist, her heart thudding in excitement. She owned an entire gold coin. All her very own. And it wasn't just any gold coin. It was a deuce, worth enough to keep her in food and a roof over her head for a month. She pressed her lips together to stifle the squeal that threatened to erupt.

Unless it was fake.

She frowned, her grip tightening automatically on her companion's waist as Ty urged his horse up a steep slope. Could gold coins be faked? When they reached the top, she released her grip and reached into her cloak.

Around her neck was a small leather pouch Ty had tossed her before they'd mounted. She'd tucked the coin inside, taking great care to knot the top before placing the lanyard around her neck. She'd seen a deuce such as this once. Not one as shiny though. Maybe this was newly minted?

She released the pouch, taking care to tuck it between her breasts before sliding her arm around Ty again. She leaned to one side, her gaze catching on the big man riding ahead of them. If he were a Realm-appointed Overseer he should have many more coins at his disposal. Maybe he could give her some sort of loan.

She shivered in remembrance of the scene in the taproom. Somehow, he didn't strike her as a person who would lend money to a woman with no means of support. With his anger tightly leashed, he was formidable. She would hate to get on his bad side.

She shuddered at the thought of him losing the rein on his control. He had a cruel face, but his gesture had been anything but cruel. With his hair as black as a raven's wing, his angular face, hooded dark brown eyes and his firm jaw, some women might find him very attractive. Not her though—

Liar...

She laid her cheek against Ty's soft cloak. Her box dug into her belly but she ignored the discomfort. She wasn't a woman to trifle with a man and she wasn't about to start now. She was on her way to an exciting new adventure and now had money of her own. While the big man seemed to think she was his slave, she would have to disabuse him of that notion. He'd be disappointed that he'd lost the money she represented, but maybe she could find a way to pay him back—

"Hold."

Beneath her cheek, she felt Ty pulling on the reins until the horse came to a jolting stop. Dani craned her neck as she leaned to the side, her breath caught in her throat as she took in the view below them.

They were on a cliff overlooking a large city. In the darkness, the lights twinkled like fairy dust along rows of neat buildings. The sudden release of tension in Ty's body made it clear that this was home to her companions. Did the big man have control of such a large place? If he did, then he truly was rich, richer than she'd suspected.

The object of her thoughts nudged his horse forward, leaving Ty and Dani to follow. A ball of anxiety formed in her stomach and expanded as they wove down the cliff and into the outskirts of the city. Dani loosened her wrap for the air was much warmer here than in the mountains. She took a deep breath and inhaled the fragrance of freshly turned earth, animals and night-blooming carnelian flowers.

They rode past small huts tucked between neat patches of fields. These properties obviously belonged to farmers and herders. Their windows were darkened, as they would be rising soon to tend to their chores.

As they approached the center of the city, the streets turned from dirt paths to gravel and finally solid white rock. Dani's neck ached from her attempts to see everything at once. The houses went from modest to outlandish within the distance of a few streets. Few people were out with the exception of the half-naked ladies who'd hung out the window of one establishment and called for Ty as they'd ridden past.

All too soon, they left the white paved streets and rode toward a massive castle, complete with turrets, drawbridge and guards. Acres of rolling land surrounded the castle walls and Dani detected the rustle of animals in the darkness. As they approached, a drawbridge lowered over the moat, welcoming them into the bailey.

After they entered, Dani heard the creaking of a great chain and she looked back as the bridge ascended once again. She swallowed hard. This place might be tricky to escape.

"Welcome home, sire."

A small man came forward and took the reins of the big man's horse. She couldn't help but admire the easy grace with which he dismounted from the animal.

"Thank you, Jax," he said. "It's good to be home."

Dani scowled as she received a not-too-gentle poke in the ribs from Ty, signaling her that it was time for her to get down. She shoved her wooden box at him for safekeeping as she dug her nails into his arm. Her feet hit the ground and her knees wobbled. She was unaccustomed to riding or sitting for any length of time and wanted more than anything to sink down to the ground. She'd be damned before she'd allow herself to fall in front of these men.

"Follow him." Ty shoved her box at her.

The big man was walking toward the towering entrance to the castle. Stumbling in his wake, Dani caught up just as he entered the door. She skidded to a halt at the sight before her.

The entrance was probably the grandest place she'd ever seen. Thick colorful carpets covered a pale stone floor and tapestries and paintings covered the towering walls. High overhead a light fixture blazed, casting a golden glow over the entire area. At the far end was a wide staircase and a woman was running toward them.

Her dark hair was tumbled about her head as if she'd just awakened. Her slender form was clad in a gauzy blue material that floated as she ran.

"You're home." She flung her arms around the big man and gave him a noisy kiss. "I'm so pleased."

He chuckled and Dani couldn't believe she'd heard the sound. Throughout the entire trip he'd been taciturn, barely uttering a single word, let alone laugh. Who was this woman? His wife? Mistress?

"You've brought good news, I hope?" she asked.

"Nay, 'twasn't her."

The woman made a soothing sound. "Don't worry, Haaken. She'll come, I know it. I feel it."

"I hope you're right, Ren."

"I always am—"

Dani turned away, pretending not to listen. But she'd turned too soon and stumbled into a small table, setting a narrow arrangement of flowers tottering. Releasing the grip on her box, it hit the floor with a crash, leaving her clutching the vase and the now disarrayed flowers.

The woman's gaze swung toward her. She blinked several times as if she couldn't quite believe what she was seeing. "Who do we have here?" she asked.

Haaken frowned at Dani. "What is your name again, girl?"

"Dani." She put the vase back in its previous position. "My name is Dani."

"How did you end up with her?" the woman asked.

"She's a long story." Haaken leaned forward, whispering to the woman.

"No!" She cast a scandalized look at Dani.

Face hot, Dani released the vase and retrieved her box. She had no idea what he'd said but she could well imagine that it hadn't been flattering.

"Why the nerve—" the woman blurted.

He shook his head and laid a finger over her mouth, stemming the flow of words. "Can you take care of her for me?"

"Oh yes, right away." She looked at Dani, her gaze assessing. "Is she to be added to your—"

"I haven't decided." Haaken walked to the steps. "Just take care of her. The hour draws late and the dawn approaches."

The woman looked at her, then made a soft humming sound. Whatever she was thinking, Dani had a feeling she wasn't going to like it.

Chapter Four

The moment Dani followed the woman through a gated doorway near the stairs, the entire atmosphere of the castle changed. Gone were the ornate furnishings and in their place was understated elegance. Thick rugs in soothing tones of peach and pale green cushioned her footfalls. The walls were ivory plaster with paintings and silk tapestries hung at regular intervals. Along the passage there were several inviting nooks with overstuffed chairs grouped for conversation.

At one point they passed a massive bank of windows that overlooked torch-lit gardens like nothing she'd ever seen in her life. It was still early in the growing season here in the southlands, but there was lush green grass and a profusion of blooms so brilliant it almost hurt her eyes. She could hardly wait to see it in the daylight.

Dani stumbled as the woman turned to the right and led her into a room with a tiled floor. The mixed scents of perfume oils and steam hung thick in the air. In the center of the room was a large pool of water surrounded by rose-colored marble benches. Steam rose from the water. At the far end of the room there were several smaller pools shrouded by drapes of white linen. Obviously intended for those who wished to bathe unobserved.

"The castle has its own natural hot springs," the woman said. She stopped in a small alcove that contained a mauve silk-covered bench. "Put your belongings here until I can find a room for you." She gave Dani a big smile. "By the way, I'm Haaken's sister, Ren."

His sister!

Oddly relieved, Dani gave her a slight smile. "It's nice to meet you, Ren. Can you tell me where I am?"

Ren blinked. "Haaken didn't tell you?" She rolled her eyes. "Men. Why does this not surprise me? This is the Overseer's castle in the city of Wryven. Haaken is the Overseer and you're to partake of his hospitality." She retrieved a silk robe from a peg on the wall. "Remove your clothes and put this on."

Dani looked at the robe suspiciously. "I don't have to take another bath, do I?"

"Well," Ren wrinkled her nose, "you do smell like a horse."

Dani looked down at her pale arms. Horse smell or not, she was cleaner now than when she'd been birthed. "I don't—"

"We'll tend your skin," she said. "Haaken told me you'd been injured." Ren set the robe on the bench and moved to leave, pulling the silk hangings free from their ties to cover the entrance to the alcove. "Just come out when you're ready and I'll get my things."

Ren left and Dani was alone. Clutching her box, she examined the small space. The alcove was undersized but luxurious with an ornate bench and a small table with a crystal lamp from which golden light spilled forth. Along one wall was a line of pegs that held various garments, most looking like robes. Did Haaken have many visitors to his baths?

She set her box on the table and removed her clothing. The rough cloth had been torture to her abused skin and she was glad to be rid of it. But, no matter how much the cloth irritated

128

her, these garments were all she had and, once her bath was over, she'd be forced to put them on again. She folded the items and created a neat stack on the bench before she removed the bag containing the coin.

Unable to resist temptation, she pulled out the coin. The gold was shiny and she ran her thumb over it. One side bore the stamp of a raven and the other the crown of the realm. She frowned and ran her thumb over the raven. Why the raven? Unease skittered down her spine. What was it about the raven that—

"Dani?"

Ren's soft voice jerked her from her musing and she stuffed the coin back into the bag before tucking it into the box with her other treasures. It should be safe enough there while she took a simple bath. She scooped up the robe, taking care that her calloused hands didn't snag the fragile lavender silk. Wrapped in the insubstantial garment, she slipped through the drapes.

Ren was crouched by one of the smaller baths and she waved Dani over. "Slip in here and relax. I've brought you some tea and sweetbreads, nothing too heavy to interrupt your sleep."

Dani eyed the water. "Is it very hot?"

"No, it will be perfect, I promise you. I've added oils—almond to soften your skin and chamomile, bay and lavender for healing." Ren held up a small vial for Dani to see. "And when you're done, we'll also oil your injuries, and by the time you wake, you'll feel like a new woman."

Dani doubted that but she was too polite to argue, so she climbed the tiled steps and dipped her toe into the water. It was warm but not overly so. As Ren turned away to prepare her tea, Dani tossed off the robe and hastened into the water.

"Each of these smaller baths has a different temperature, with the coldest being in the far corner surrounded by the blue tile and the hottest with the red." Ren set the tray where Dani could reach it. "I don't recommend the hot one." She grinned.

Dani settled into the water on a low seat built into one of the narrow ends of the tub. The water was heavenly against her sore body and the scent of the oils was calming.

"I'm going to fix your hair." Ren approached with a comb and silver shears. Her nose wrinkled. "They made quite a mess, didn't they?"

Dani didn't know if they had or not as she hadn't seen what had been done to her, but she'd felt the odd tufts that stuck up on her head as they'd ridden. From the tray by her arm, she selected a tart and bit into the crunchy crust, closing her eyes in delight.

"They're good, aren't they?" Ren settled behind her. "Our cook makes lemon for me as they're my favorite."

The women settled into a companionable silence that was punctuated by the soft whisk of shears. A short while later when Ren had pronounced herself done, Dani was surprised to see that the tray was bare with the exception of some crumbs and her teacup was empty as well. She was truly replete, something she'd not felt very often in her life.

Ren patted her on the shoulder. "Your bath is almost done and your hair looks much better."

"Thank you," Dani said.

"My pleasure." Ren retrieved her tray of vials from a low table nearby. "jaJin will be here to aid you with your bath while I prepare your room."

"Who is jaJin?" Dani frowned. "I can bathe on my own—"

"'Tis customary for the women of the house of Wryven to be bathed." Ren shrugged. "'Tis our way."

"I'm not a woman of—"

"You are now." Ren gave her a secretive smile.

As the other woman left, Dani leaned her head back and allowed her eyes to slip closed. Just how many *women* were there? Two? Dozens? She wanted to ask but suddenly she felt so weary, her tongue almost thick and it didn't seem to want to cooperate with her. She sighed. When she'd ridden out of her father's life, she'd never imagined people lived in such luxury.

She giggled. If they could see her now, they'd be green with jealousy. Sitting naked in warm scented water up to her chin. Indulging in more food than she'd ever seen in her life and surrounded by luxuries the likes of which she'd never dreamed. And Haaken, oh my. There was a man who would set a woman's heart to flutter with just a look. He'd certainly set something to flutter in her, something she'd never experienced before.

The sound of footsteps interrupted her musing. A cool breeze touched her cheeks as the curtain was opened then slid shut. Through her lowered lashes, she saw a slim, dark figure move around the tub. She was so tired, she just couldn't seem to bring herself to open her eyes. Sometimes, it was just easier to...accept.

Gentle hands slipped under her head and adjusted the soft support that cushioned her neck from the edge of the tub. Murmuring her thanks, she remained in the welcoming twilight world as someone—jaJin, she supposed—took a cloth and gently bathed her face and neck with the scented water. As the bathing progressed, she drifted on a cloud of sensation. A languid movement of water, then someone sat at her feet, attending to parts previously untouched.

Talented hands massaged her calves, working their way up to her aching thighs. She groaned as her silent jaJin worked the knots from her limbs until her legs were splayed open, limp. Cloth-covered fingers stroked the inside of her thighs before they moved upward, parting her flesh to be cleansed.

She whimpered as the nubby cloth was drawn over her ultra-sensitive skin and a trill of feeling danced over her skin. Entranced but untutored, Dani shifted her hips to follow the sensation. The movement was repeated again, then again. Each gentle pass drawing a sigh from her as feelings intensified. Her nipples beaded and her hands curled over the edge of the tub as the hand stroked her needy flesh.

Dimly, she was aware that she shouldn't be allowing such shocking liberties with her body. But she was so relaxed and it felt so good that she couldn't form a coherent protest. Nor did she want to. A soapy hand stroked her erect nipples, first one then the other as the first hand continued its sensual assault. Tension spiraled higher and her gut clenched as wave after wave of sensation washed over her skin. Her body arched and she cried out as movement quickened and then, with one final stroke, she was...free.

Dani sagged against the tub, her breathing ragged. She sighed as the hands left her. If this was what happened every time the women of Wryven bathed, no wonder the baths were so large. She was surprised the women ever left.

The image of Haaken's face rose in her mind's eye. Big, strong, his bronzed skin dampened from the bath as he—

Wait, what was she doing? She frowned. Now why would he come to mind now? Haaken was handsome, yes, but he was also overbearing—

Sexy...

Autocratic—

Has a smile that would make a woman's knees go weak...

A slow tingle ignited between her thighs and she blinked open her eyes. A slim blond man stood by the tub arranging fresh towels. He wore something that resembled a white loincloth and it was wet.

Soaking wet.

Her gaze danced away and she gulped. jaJin was a man and he'd been in the tub with her! Heat seared her cheeks. She'd allowed a man, a complete stranger, to touch her as no man ever had before. *Oh Ola, what have I done?*

His gaze met hers and, in his soft golden brown eyes, there was no leer. No lust, just understanding. He waited as Dani crouched in the bottom of the tub. After what she'd allowed him to do, could she exit the tub in front of this man?

He didn't say anything, but he seemed to understand her quandary. He picked up a large towel and held it out, averting his eyes as if to say it was okay for her to come out now.

Mustering her courage, Dani rose on rubbery legs and snatched the towel from him, then wrapped it around herself. As she stepped from the tub, he made no move to touch her. With a gesture of his hand, he indicated that she was to sit on a small bench next to the tub. After she was seated, she noticed something else about jaJin.

He was erect.

Very erect.

She averted her eyes from his loincloth to his graceful hands as he picked up a small bottle and a cloth. Dribbling the liquid from the bottle onto the cloth, he attended to her injuries, wiping the cool liquid over each mark left by her rough handlers the day before.

When he'd attended to all of the areas that weren't covered by her towel, he handed her the bottle and then turned away, allowing Dani to tend to those wounds herself.

After she was done, he retrieved her robe, turning away once again to allow her privacy as she dressed. As she fumbled with the garment, she heard a loud gasp from behind her. Dani hastily wrapped the robe shut and turned to see Ren entering, a look of shock on her face.

"Dani—"

jaJin stepped around her and shook his head at Ren, silencing her.

"What's wrong?" Dani shook her head. She was feeling muzzy-headed again.

"Nothing, we'll talk in the morning." Ren gave her a wide smile as she approached, sliding her arm through Dani's. "Come, I'll take you to your room."

"My stuff—"

"jaJin will have it sent up with one of the guards. Don't worry." Ren gave her a friendly squeeze. "All will be just *excellent* now."

Dani allowed the other woman to lead her from the baths. The path they took was long and winding and she felt sure she'd never find her way back. Ren led her up a towering set of steps, the soft carpet cushioning her dragging feet.

She barely had time to notice the sumptuous appointments before Ren helped her from the robe and she was ushered into the bed. Silk bed coverings slithered against and soothed her skin and she yawned so hard she felt like her face would split. The scent of carnelian flowers scented the air as Dani closed her eyes and fell asleep.

Haaken stared at the sleeping woman. It couldn't be. It was impossible. This woman was a traveler *slave*, not even born high enough to be considered a common-born woman by anyone in the realm. His sister had to be mistaken, that was the only answer.

She lay on her side on the peach-colored silk sheets. Ren had shorn her hair to a uniform, if very short, length. Her features were delicate, almost fey in repose. She had a small, upturned nose, pale brows and lashes and a mouth so rosy it reminded him of fresh Sladerian berries still warm from the fields. He wondered what she would taste like.

But, a traveler?

Pushing the thought away, he pulled down the sheet that covered her. As each inch was revealed, the tender curve of her back, the slight indentation of her spine and finally, the gentle curve of her buttocks, the heat in his groin built to a near painful level. His heart stopped. There, on the base of her spine just above her soft curves, was what he sought. His hand shook as he saw the small birthmark resembling a raven's claw.

She was The One.

Chapter Five

The sound of falling water was lulling her to sleep. Dani stretched, enjoying the novelty of thick grass still warm from the setting sun. Here in the south, the seasons had just turned and the time of planting was upon them. In the north, where her family remained, it would still be cold for many weeks yet.

She frowned at the disturbing thought of her family. She'd been living in Wryven for almost a week now. One whole week of fresh plentiful food and a pile of new clothing. Not a single garment had been worn before, not even once. Then there were the reading and writing lessons, which she was enjoying immensely. The best part was no one ordered her around or tried to grab her inappropriately.

Unless she wanted to be grabbed, of course.

Her cheeks heated at the thought of jaJin and her first hours in the castle. She wasn't sure what disturbed her more—allowing jaJin scandalous access to her body or the heated dreams of Haaken that had occurred every night since her arrival. She shivered.

As Ren insisted, Dani allowed jaJin to assist her while bathing, but she never again allowed him the liberties as she had that first evening. According to her new friend, a sexually fulfilled woman was a happy and contented one. All of the high-born Wryven women had access to the jaJin, or the Pleasure

Bearers as they were known, and, from what Dani could tell, they made good use of them.

Three other women resided in the castle besides the servants and Ren. From what she'd gathered, they were concubines to the Overseer though she'd never seen Haaken with any of them. Ty was another story. He seemed to spend quite a bit of time with the ladies, laughing and flirting outrageously.

When not attending to Ty, the ladies spent most of their time lazing around the baths and indulging themselves with the jaJin. KayLe, the older dark-haired one, had taken an immediate dislike to Dani though she wasn't sure why as she'd barely spoken with her.

She opened her eyes and glanced to her left. Along the tree line, she spied the familiar hunk of her shadow, Mik. From the moment she woke to the moment she entered her bedchamber, she was under constant surveillance by the Wryven warrior. Dani wasn't sure why she had a guard; the other women didn't have one. Was it because Haaken feared she'd flee and he'd lose his investment? Judging from the obvious wealth of the castle, the amount he'd paid for her had been a mere pittance of his worth.

She rolled onto her belly, her chin coming to rest on her wrist. Whatever the reason for Mik's presence, she was growing weary of the constant surveillance and her lack of duties. How did Wryven women stand the boredom? She needed something to do besides her lessons, deciding what to wear and eating all day. She grinned. Of course, eating all day did have its benefits as she'd gained a few pounds.

She yawned. Maybe she'd venture to the kitchens and see if the cook had made more lemon tarts. Then again, Ren had told her not to eat too much as there was a special banquet tonight, late tonight—

A soft trill of laughter brought her head up in time to see Ren run across the cropped grass with a bundle in her arms. She tossed back her mane of dark hair and laughed. Close on her heels was a large man dressed in full Wryven uniform. He towered over his slight prey, but Ren didn't seem worried.

Was this the mysterious Lorn that Ren had mentioned? A top-level commander in Wryven's security forces, Ren had high hopes that her brother would grant them permission to marry soon.

Dani grinned and rolled to her feet. From what little Ren had told her, Lorn was a man with the stamina of a horse, the heart of a lion and the face of an angel. Burning with curiosity, she could hardly wait to see this man in the flesh.

She darted across the grass and onto the wooded path that Ren and her companion had used. Thick overhead branches kept the trail perpetually sheltered from the sun and the air was cool and moist. She followed the narrow path to a cozy sheltered spot overlooking a steaming pool of water surrounded by glowing torches.

Ren and the warrior stood on a large flat rock and he was disrobing, his eyes locked on the lovely woman before him. Ren took his discarded garments and folded them, laying them neatly to the side. Dani's eyes widened as she stared at the now-bare warrior. He was massive, every inch of him hard muscles and sun-browned skin. She'd never seen a naked male before. At least none completely bare and certainly none who looked like him.

Ren tipped back her head and favored him with a wicked smile. "Shall I perform the services of a jaJin?"

He gave a rumbling laugh. "Whatever gave you that idea?"

The warrior looked down and Dani saw his erect staff standing proudly from a thatch of thick, dark hair. She gulped. She'd never seen a cock the size of his either. The only cock she'd ever seen had been a fellow traveler's several years back. She'd been foraging and she'd come upon him relieving himself. His cock had been a short, stubby limp thing. Nothing at all like this majestic occurrence before her now.

"This big man right here." Ren reached for him, her fingers curling around the shaft of his cock.

His head tipped back and he groaned as she stroked his flesh. Was she hurting him? Ren pushed the unresisting warrior onto a smooth rock, her fingers never releasing his hard flesh. Ren sank to her knees between his spread legs.

Dani's eyes grew wide as she watched her friend put her mouth to the bulbous head. Lorn shifted his hips, pressing toward her mouth. His big hand cupped her head as she moved her mouth up and down on his cock. His muscles flexed with each movement and he moaned when she cupped his testicles with her other hand.

Dani sank into a low crouch, fascinated with what she saw. What would it be like to have a man under her power like this? Did it feel as powerful as it looked? An image of Haaken, naked and at her command, caused a shiver of awareness to race down her spine. What would it be like to take Haaken into her mouth...his big body straining beneath her as she sucked him—

A guttural cry pulled her from her mouth-watering fantasy. Lorn had collapsed against the rock, his big body coated with sweat. Ren released his cock, then climbed up onto the rock-seat next to him. He gave her a satisfied smile as he slid an arm around her. She laid her head on his shoulder and his hand lazily stroked her back.

Even from fifteen feet away, Dani could feel the tenderness between the two of them. After a few moments of shared silence, they spoke in low whispers as they shared numerous kisses. This was more than the raw sex she'd witnessed around the castle. Was this love? What would it feel like to be held in a man's arms and share secrets of the heart?

Uneasy, she backed away. Did all men behave as such with their mates? What about Haaken and his concubines? Disturbed by the thought, she moved to return the way she'd come. She needed some time and space to come to grips with what she'd witnessed. When she turned, a shadow loomed over her. Her heart stopped, a scream caught in her throat.

A massive warrior blocked her escape. For a split second, she was a small child again being tossed into the streets by the Malian guard. A feeling of helplessness came over her and she shrank backward, no longer afraid that Ren would see her. She was more concerned with evading the warrior.

The figure reached up and Dani flinched. He stilled, then moved slowly to remove his helm. Long, silky black hair tumbled out, followed by a strong jaw and a mouth that haunted her dreams. A strong nose and dark eyes with heavy brows followed to create a face that threatened to stop her heart.

"Haaken." Her voice sounded faint to her own ears.

"Dani, are you well?"

She nodded, relieved that it was him, yet mortified that she'd been having illicit thoughts about him only moments before.

"What are you doing here?" he asked.

"I was—"

A splash sounded from the pool and it brought Haaken forward. He placed his big hands on her shoulders and leaned around her to see through the dense growth. With her nose so close to his chest, she inhaled his masculine scent of leather and warm flesh. A shiver of awareness slithered down her spine.

"I see."

Dani couldn't tell if he was angry that his sister was trysting with her lover. She looked up and their gazes clashed. His eyes were fixed on her mouth. Suddenly nervous, she dampened her lips. Her heartbeat accelerated as he raised his hand and brushed his thumb along the edge of her lower lip.

More than anything she wanted to feel his mouth against hers. To experience the slow slide of his tongue, the heat of his arms encircling her as their mouths mated. As his head dipped toward hers, a sudden spurt of nervousness had her blurting out, "She loves him."

"Indeed." The spell broken, he dropped his hand. "And what do you know of love, little one?"

She shrugged. "I admit I don't know much of love but I know Ren is far more worldly than I, and when she says that she's in love, I believe her."

"Women," Haaken snorted. "Your logic never fails to astound me."

Stung, she moved around him toward the trail and the manicured gardens adjoining the castle. While she'd been spying on Ren and her lover, the sun had set and the stars were coming out.

"Come, let us not fight." He caught her easily and took her hand in his. His fingers were calloused and warm as they slipped around her wrist. "I've returned from inspecting my lands and I brought you something. I also desire a conversation with you."

Dani fell into step beside him, secretly enjoying the lazy way his thumb stroked the inside of her wrist. "What do you want to speak with me about?"

"Your past and your—"

"You've arrived!"

KayLe ran toward them and Dani felt jealousy burn low in her gut. The older woman's hair was raven black and it was arranged in an intricate series of braids and loops that resembled a crown. Her lush figure was clad in sheer purple and fuchsia silk and she reached them in a fragrant wave of carnelian flower essence and the jangle of golden bracelets. The woman flung herself at Haaken and he was forced to release Dani's hand. Dani stepped aside to avoid being kicked.

"I missed you, sire."

Haaken gave a short laugh. "So I see."

His hands landed on her hips and Dani turned away. It was obvious that they needed to be alone. Why had he even bothered to find her in the first place?

"Hold up, Dani," Haaken called.

She turned as he removed KayLe's arms from around his shoulders. Her hands looked small and slim in his as he leaned down and whispered something before releasing KayLe and walking toward Dani.

"When will you come to me?" KayLe called.

"Later," he said.

Dani scowled at Haaken's back as she followed him into the castle. As their Overseer appeared, the servants stopped in their tracks, bowing their heads as he walked by. He appeared not to notice while Dani was fascinated. She'd never seen anything like it, this blind adoration of their master. Judging from what little she'd seen of the lands surrounding the castle, Haaken was a generous Overseer to his people.

Her bare feet made no sound on the cool tiles as they walked toward the wing that housed the family. Ren had given her an extensive tour after Dani had expressed her fear of getting lost. She'd learned that Ty and Ren had suites on the second floor while Haaken's were on the third. This was the one place she hadn't ventured.

Underfoot was deep red tile which contrasted with the white plaster walls and ceiling that soared at least fifteen feet overhead. Mahogany inlays broke the monotony of the white as this was the first place in the castle that had a complete lack of adornment. No tapestries, no paintings, no wall coverings. Just white walls and dark wood.

Torches burned at regular intervals casting the closed doorways into shadow. The overall effect was somber, unlike the rest of the castle with its ample windows and bright sunlight. She glanced at his back. How could he stand it up here?

At the far end of the hall was the only open door. The moment they entered the room, her gaze locked on a towering stained glass window. Her eyes widened. She'd seen stained glass before, but never up close and nothing quite like this.

In the center panel was a massive black raven perched on a branch. Around one leg was a golden chain with the other end attached to the branch. In the left panel was a woman clad in a black cape, her fingers old and crippled and they appeared to be casting a spell on the raven in the center panel. In the right panel was a young woman, her face obscured by a white cape. Her hands were outstretched and hovering just over her palms was a heart with lines radiating outward.

Her gaze shifted to the bottom panel. Two people, a man and the woman in the white cape, walked hand in hand. Her cape lay in a pile on the ground next to a broken gold chain.

"What do you think of it?" he asked.

"It's beautiful." She looked at him, his handsome face highlighted by a beam of moonlight piercing a jeweled red section of glass. "I've never seen anything like it. What does it mean?"

"It's a Wryven fairy tale." He turned away as his valet appeared to help him remove his clothes. "I'll tell you about it sometime."

The valet unbuckled the leather vest and removed it. Beneath Dani saw a leather jerkin that was molded to his magnificent chest.

She jerked her eyes away. "Why not tell me now?"

"I have something I'd much rather do."

Her stomach fluttered as he strode closer, pausing only to pick up a small leather pouch from a table. He opened it and she caught the flash of light on something gold.

"For you."

Dani gaped at the object that dangled from his fingertips. It was larger than a bracelet and made of links that moved against his fingers like silk, or chain mail.

"You've given me enough as it is." Indeed he had. Not a day had gone by that she hadn't received some sort of offering from him. A flower, a small book of Wryven poetry, a length of pale blue silk had been lying on her bed this afternoon. Though this was the first gift she'd received directly from his hand.

"I enjoy giving presents to beautiful women."

Dani blushed and ducked her head. "What is it?"

"It's for your ankle, to cover your scar."

She glanced down at her bare ankle and the ring of reddish-scarred flesh. It was a constant reminder of her years of captivity at the hands of her father. Did Haaken mean to bind her as well?

She raised her head, her jaw firm. "I'm no man's slave."

His brow rose. "Have I said you were?"

"I know you believe I was their slave, but I wasn't."

He took her hand and led her toward a velvet-covered stool and steered her onto it. "How did you end up there, Dani?"

Her lip trembled and she looked away. Could she tell this man that it was her father, her own flesh and blood, who'd sought to enslave her and had ultimately sold her to the highest bidder? It was too much to bear. The words could not be spoken out loud, not yet.

"It's a long story."

Haaken crouched, his fingers touched her ankle and a hot shudder of desire raced through her. He placed her bare foot upon his thigh and she could feel the heat of his skin through his leather trousers. The slide of the heated gold was almost sinful against her skin as he slipped on the anklet.

"We have all the time in the world." His fingers stroked the back of her calf, the movement sensual and hypnotic. She longed to close her eyes and revel in his attentions.

"Do we?" Her voice was thick. "Have all the time in the world?"

"You do not trust me?" His talented fingers stroked the back of one calf then he picked up her other ankle and placed her foot against his other thigh to repeat the process.

"I don't know you, Haaken." Her voice was heavy. "How can I trust you if I barely know you?" Her thighs felt terribly weak and the cleft at the apex of her legs was wet and aching.

"Fair enough." He shifted closer and her thighs parted with the movement of his legs. "What do you want me to do, Dani?"

Kiss me...

"I'm not sure what you mean." Flustered, she tried to draw her knees together.

Haaken leaned back, his expression satisfied. "You are truly an innocent, aren't you?" He removed her feet from his thighs before he rose. A large bulge in the area of his codpiece proclaimed his arousal. "I was afraid that, as a traveler, you'd be jaded."

His words shook the sensual daze from her senses. She leapt to her feet and glared at him. "You thought I'd be a whore. Not all traveler women earn their keep on their backs."

He held up his hands as if to ask for forgiveness. "I implied no such thing. I know what it is to live on the road. Those who do have a tendency to come face to face with the unsavory side of life. I'm pleased to see you're still innocent enough to enjoy the simpler pleasures of life." He took her hand and pressed a kiss to her knuckles, his mouth warm and firm. "Now, go get dressed for dinner. The cooks have prepared a feast."

"As you wish."

Disconcerted, she moved away from him, missing his heat almost immediately. The tiny bells on her anklet rang merrily as she moved. Feeling his gaze upon her, she forced herself into a sedate walk as she left his room, her heart in her throat.

A trickle of sweat ran down his back as Dani left. She was his to do with as he pleased and he couldn't prevent the thrill of possession every time he looked at her. Whatever she wanted to call it, she was his slave and his Chosen One. Either way, she was his and his alone.

He tipped his head back, his groin aching with unfulfilled lust. A single touch of her silky skin brought him to arousal. He was a man well-used to regular sexual encounters, and this had never happened before, not even when he was an untried youth.

Since the discovery of her mark, prophecy called for a fortnight of abstinence on both sides but he couldn't wait that long. Thanks to Mik, he knew she'd been completely chaste for the past week, as had he. But that would end...tonight.

"Sire, shall I draw your bath?" his valet asked.

"Yes, and make it cold." Haaken opened his eyes and looked at the moonglow spilling in through the colored panes of the raven window. "Ice cold."

Chapter Six

Dani had never felt more exposed in her life as she followed Ren into the banquet hall.

After leaving Haaken earlier that evening, she'd made her escape to the baths, hoping to find Ren and impart to her what had happened. Instead she'd found several jaJin waiting with orders to service her every need.

She'd been bathed from head to toe, then a female jaJin had come forward and shaved the hair from her legs and under her arms. She had noticed that all Wryven women were clean-shaven and she'd come to appreciate the custom. The genital shaving had surprised her, though.

All the excess hair had been removed, leaving only a narrow strip of pale curls behind. And if that wasn't enough to be endured, the woman had dyed Dani's nipples and the bottoms of her feet bright red. When asked why, the jaJin had only given her a limpid stare and said it was customary.

Dani had come to the conclusion that the Wryven had some very odd customs.

After she'd been bathed, trimmed and dyed within an inch of her life, two jaJins had rubbed a blend of carnelian and almond oil into every pore of her skin. Only then had she been deemed ready and another servant had arrived with her clothing.

But these weren't the clothes she'd come to know and appreciate.

Her undergarments were nonexistent. Around her waist was a jeweled chain with a leather strap attached in the center with more jewels placed at intervals. The strap was passed between her thighs, parting her nether lips, and then fastened in the back. As she walked, a blood red ruby stimulated the sheltered bundle of nerves while another jewel, a large sapphire, teased her damp opening, causing her to tilt her hips ever so slightly to alleviate the sensation as she walked.

Her unbound breasts swayed under layers of lavender silk that comprised her wrap-style dress. Before leaving her chamber, she'd peered in the mirror to make sure her scarlet nipples were indiscernible through the soft cloth. Never had she felt so exposed yet aroused at the same time.

The hall was packed with hundreds of people all in their finest clothing. As they passed, those in attendance bowed their heads in deference to Ren's position in the family. The tables were decorated with elaborate place settings and were piled high with food. Multiple bottles of wine were afforded each table, and judging from the flushed cheeks, many had partaken already.

As they progressed, Dani looked for a vacant spot to slip into. As a non-Wryven citizen, she would be relegated to sit on the far side of the room near the front where all visitors were to be seated. She saw an empty chair and moved to take it when Ren grabbed her sleeve.

"Where are you going?" she hissed.

"To sit—"

"You're sitting with us."

Ty was already waiting at the head table and he stood as they approached. He looked handsome in a dark blue velvet tunic with a white ruffled silk shirt beneath it. "Sister dear." He gave Ren's dark hair a tweak, then pulled her chair out for her.

"Brother, I do believe you almost have your company manners on." Ren slid into her chair as she gave him a lofty smile. "What brought this on?"

Ty pulled out a chair for Dani. "I believe it was seeing the lovely Dani again." He gestured for her to sit. "I find myself without words."

"As if that could ever happen," Dani muttered. "You, sir, have the glibbest tongue I've ever heard." She sank into her chair, shivering as the ruby nudged her. She leaned back and the sapphire teased her damp opening. Damn, was there no way to sit properly with this wretched thing on?

Ren snickered as she ducked her head to smooth her napkin across her lap. "Careful, brother, for she's grown claws since last you saw her."

"Ah, I think you underestimate her." Ty reclaimed his seat. "You failed to notice that she had claws all along. She chose to shield them."

Ren gave her an approving smile. "A smart woman never reveals all her armaments."

Ty leaned over. "And you will do well to remember that, young Dani, for that piece of knowledge will serve you well."

A blast of trumpets interrupted their conversation and the footman stepped forward.

"Ladies and gentleman." His voice carried easily through the large hall. "Please stand for the arrival of our Overseer, Count Haaken el dan Wryven."

Dani scrambled to her feet as he entered with his two lieutenants at his heels. His gaze swept the crowd before coming to rest on the head table, then upon her.

Heat flowed through her body as his gaze moved over her. She fought the urge to squirm beneath his appreciative glance. Between the jewels and Haaken, she could only pray she'd escape without making a complete fool of herself before the hundreds in attendance.

With his dark hair loose about his shoulders and dressed in black from head to toe, he looked enormous. The only color to break the unrelenting length and breadth of him was a royal purple sash about his slim waist. A jeweled dagger was tucked into the sash. He moved with an easy grace, a man at home within his skin.

"Sit." He spoke to her as he mounted the dais.

Dani assumed her seat, trying to hide her discomfort as the jewels made their presence known. Only when she was seated did he too sit, as did the rest of the diners. A robed priest entered the room with several children trailing behind him. He stopped before the main table and opened a large book.

Dani was disappointed when he spoke to the assembled crowd in a language she didn't understand. Every few moments, the priest would stop and the crowd would shout something in response to his words.

"They're agreeing." Haaken's voice sounded in her ear.

"To what?"

"To his questions. Soon, he will ask you a question as well. All you have to say is 'oret-ah' which means 'I agree'."

"What if I don't agree?" Dani hissed. "I don't even know what he's saying—"

The crowd gave a tremendous roar and surged to their feet. The priest turned to face the head table and the children came forward. Dani saw they each carried a small wreath on a royal purple pillow.

The priest addressed a question to Ren and Ty. With solemn expressions, they both responded with "oret-ah" and the children placed wreaths of white flowers on their heads and the crowds cheered.

Dani frowned as Haaken was next. The only word she could make out was his name but the gesture toward her was unmistakable. Haaken gave the expected response and the hall erupted into cheers again as a slightly larger wreath of white flowers was placed on his head.

The crowd settled and Dani could feel thousands of eyes fixed upon her. The priest spoke and she could only pick out her name. When he stopped speaking, the silence was heavy, almost unbearable.

"Oret-ah?"

The crowd erupted into wild shouts of delight at her whispered word. The priest made the sign of the Realm, then closed the book. A young girl came forward and Dani dipped her head to receive the wreath. The girl gave her a shy smile as she backed away.

Haaken caught her hand and raised it to his lips. His look was approving as he kissed her knuckles and a shiver moved up her arm. He kept her hand in his as he gestured and the servers entered the room bearing large trays heaped with food. The banquet had begun.

"You look breathtaking." His breath was warm against her ear. Through the thin silk she could feel the heat that radiated off him.

"'Tis your custom that dictated my outfit." She picked up her wineglass. Did he know what she wore beneath her dress? She took a gulp of the golden liquid.

"Aye, 'tis custom."

Dani choked and Haaken patted her on the back until her coughing ceased. She smiled her thanks, grateful when a question from Ren took Haaken's attention away from her. Throughout the hall, the guests were served and their chatter had risen to a dull roar, but she didn't miss the curious glances being sent her way. To her left was a table where the concubines were seated, KayLe included. Had Haaken visited her after she'd left? The other woman's hungry gaze was fastened on the Overseer.

Her dark gaze slid to Dani and her eyes narrowed. She picked up her meat knife and speared a large meat shank. After she removed a chunk, she bit into it, a drop of meat juice running down her chin.

Dani looked away.

"Something vexes you?" Haaken asked.

"No. Just tired."

"'Tis late for you, little one." He reached for a meat trencher and selected a small roasted bird. "Come, let us eat and you'll feel much better." He tore a piece off the roasted bird and offered it to her.

Dani made to take it from him and he moved his hand, not allowing her to do so. His gaze was fastened on her mouth and he raised the morsel to her lips. Slowly, she leaned forward and took the proffered bite from his fingertips. The meat was tender and juicy, seasoned to perfection, but Dani was having trouble swallowing with his gaze fixed on her. Was this seduction?

From the platter of glazed fruits, she selected a luscious slice of tropiel, a citrus fruit. She bit into it before offering Haaken the other half. His eyes glowed with approval as he leaned forward and took the fruit, his tongue lingering long enough to remove the juice from her fingertips.

Their meal turned into a sensual byplay of give and take. Not a word was spoken as they fed each other bite after bite. The hundreds of guests faded into the background as they lost themselves in each other. All too soon, Dani was full and the emptied trenchers were removed. As the last plate was taken away, dancers took center stage.

She'd never seen anything like the women who'd taken the floor. Their floating skirts were of every color imaginable and trimmed in gold or silver. They all had long dark hair and heavily lined dark eyes. Their breasts were bare and thin chains hung from their erect nipples. With stunning footwork and incredible contortions of their nubile bodies, they dazzled everyone in the room.

As the ladies completed their dance, Dani felt a light brush of skin across her wrist. Haaken looked down at her, his eyes burned with need. Wordlessly, he held his hand out toward her. She licked her lips, as her heart beat a wild tattoo. Taking her future in her own hands, Dani slipped her hand into his and together they left the hall, never looking back.

Haaken was hard as a rock when they stepped outside into the darkness. As he led Dani into the moonlight, he rubbed his thumb over the back of her hand, marveling at the softness of her skin. The Tuli-tay, or mating feast, continued in the hall behind them. The sword dancers now taking the floor and the copious amounts of free-flowing wine would keep the attendees busy until dawn.

Just as he would keep his mate busy until dawn.

Not that Dani knew she was his mate. The situation was too complicated to try and get her to understand it as his time was running out. The ritual feast had to take place tonight along with their mating ritual. In a few months, when she knew him better and had adjusted to the idea of a life in Wryven, he could explain the urgency of his actions to her.

"This isn't the way to my room." Dani tugged on his hand as he led her toward a secret entrance to the family wing.

"You aren't going to your room."

"I'm not?" Her tone was bemused. "Where am I going?"

"To mine."

She stumbled against his arm. "Don't I have any say in this?" He heard the tone of annoyance in her voice, overlaid with a quiver of excitement.

Haaken stopped so fast she stumbled into him again. He turned and their gazes clashed. "Of course you have a say. But I'm warning you now, if you object, you'd better make your objections known now as I can't guarantee that I'll be able to stop later."

He could see the indecision on her face. Oh, what he would give to be able to read her mind at this moment. Dani's chest rose and fell with each ragged breath and her nipples were hard. She bit her lower lip then gave him a slight nod. Jubilant, he swept her into his arms, her anklet giving a merry ring. He knew the back tunnels of the castle like a map of his own face. He walked through a small archway and into the darkness. He didn't need torches to light his way as he wove through a series of halls and staircases. The only light afforded them were intermittent patches of moonlight on the floors beneath the windows.

She was small and warm in his arms. Her skin fragrant. He'd seen her red feet. Had they rouged her nipples as well? His blood heated at the thought. What was it about Dani that made him want to lose control as he did? All of his life women had been plentiful. As a thirteenth generation Overseer for the Realm, he held power and luxury in his palm. Both were powerful aphrodisiacs and it had attracted women to the house of Wryven in droves. He'd partaken in his share of the ladies, enjoying their company and the sensual delights of their bodies. But none had invaded his mind like the one in his arms.

He ducked his head and walked through the doorway and into his bedchamber. The massive bed, the same bed where generations of Wryven rulers had been conceived and born, had been moved directly beneath the towering stained glass window, throwing patches of color on the white silk sheets. A low fire crackled, illuminating the bottle of wine and assortment of cheeses awaiting their pleasure.

He moved to the bed, then released his grip on her legs, allowing her to slide down his body. Her luminous eyes widened as his cock nudged her belly. He stroked the soft skin of her arms, then moved to her back. She relaxed into him, her arms sliding around his waist.

He slid his hand along her neck and tilted her chin upward. His lips brushed hers, then moved in for a lingering touch. He savored the texture of her skin, the taste of her mouth. Hesitant, she opened beneath him as his tongue slid along her lower lip then dipped inside. He cupped the back of her head, reveling in the feel of his mate in his arms, her heated mouth open to his.

Their tongues tangled as he taught her how to kiss. Soon she proved herself to be an adept student when she nipped his lower lip. His blood surged at the feel of her teeth.

Too soon...

She needed more time to accept him as a woman accepts her man.

He abandoned her mouth, his tongue zeroing in on the spot at the base of her throat where her pulse beat frantically. The tie of her dress tickled his ear as he laved attention upon her.

Her head tipped back as he caught one end tie with his teeth and gave it a gentle tug.

The silk held, then slithered apart, baring her to the waist. He heard her gasp and she grabbed for the cloth, but he caught her wrists, halting her movement.

"Don't cover yourself." His voice was hoarse. "You're beautiful and I want to see you."

She quit resisting and he released her. Her breasts were beautiful—small but perfectly formed. And, to his delight, her nipples were rouged scarlet. He slid his hand over a soft globe, plumping it as his thumb teased her nipple. Her breath caught and he repeated the movement, watching as it hardened even further. He moved in and took her nipple into his mouth to tease with his tongue. She moaned, her fingers fisting in his hair, holding him tight to her breast.

His blood surged at her tight grip and he switched breasts, suckling hard as her breathy cries urged him on. His hands dropped to her waist, finding the tie that held her dress. Beneath the silk he could feel the jeweled belt and his cock thrust against his codpiece. He was so hard it was becoming painful to keep himself confined.

He tugged on the tie and her dress came free, sliding to the floor. He picked her up and laid her on the bed, taking only a second to admire her pale form against the paler sheets before joining her. Her nipples stood in sharp contrast to her body, their tips red and damp from his mouth. Dressed only in the jeweled girdle and the gold anklet, she was a sight to make any man weak in the knees.

He teased her nipples, alternating between biting and sucking, before he kissed a leisurely path down her stomach. The belt rode low on her hips, the gems gleaming in the semi-darkness. On the front of the belt was a small loop. He slid his finger through it and gave the belt an experimental tug.

Dani gave a surprised cry and she grabbed for him. "What—"

"Shh. Close your eyes." He waited until she did as he requested. "Now, just feel."

He gave the belt a slight tug and she whimpered, her fingers twisting in the sheets. He pressed her thighs together, knowing the friction would be greater. He pulled on the loop and her hips followed his direction, thrusting against the jewels. He settled into an easy rhythm, her sighs and gasps setting the pace of his movements. Her driving hips increased their pace with each tug of the leather and when she cried out, the sound was muffled by her own fist in her mouth.

She was limp as he parted her thighs and removed the belt, catching a glimpse of her damp inner flesh. She was now ready for her mate.

Shaking, he rose and stripped off his clothes, his gaze never leaving her soft curves as they lay spread across his bed in a banquet of femininity. He covered her, taking her mouth with a savage hunger, and she met him, stroke for stroke. His stomach clenched as she rolled her hips beneath him and his cock tightened to an almost unbearable level.

He left her mouth for a taste of her nipples. Her soft pleas sounded as he suckled first one then the other. He nibbled a trail of heat down her stomach, ending at her neatly trimmed thatch. He parted her damp flesh and blew against the sensitive bundle of nerves. She arched at the blast of air and gave an agonized cry.

That sound almost threw him over the edge. He felt pre-come dampen the head of his cock. He thought he could wait, but he was wrong. He had to have her, now.

He rose, pressing his cock between her thighs, torturing himself by rubbing against her damp lips. So close and yet so far. She was trembling, arching beneath him as he mastered her flesh, raising his and her arousal to a near fevered pitch.

He gripped her backside in his hands, spreading her legs to accommodate him better. He knelt for a second and looked down. At where her damp flesh and pale curls touched the head of his cock. The moment he entered her, they would be bound and their lives would never be the same.

With a thrust of his hips, he buried himself in her heat. He felt her cry, the slight resistance that proclaimed her innocence, but he was too far gone. He covered her tense body, bracing his upper body on his arms. The urge to thrust himself into oblivion was strong and it was only by the slimmest of measure that he managed to restrain himself. He wouldn't go alone, he'd take her with him or die trying.

He spread his legs, forcing her thighs farther apart, exposing her delicate nodule to every movement of his cock. Fully open beneath him, he thrust slowly until the tension left her body and she began moving with him.

His body automatically fell into its natural rhythm, each movement increasing the tension as he thrust deeper, longer into her flesh. As the blood pounded in his ears, he heard her breathy cries and could feel her straining beneath him. At the first caress of her release, a pleasure so intense washed over him that it sucked the breath from his lungs and all feeling from his extremities. As wave after wave of release washed over him, he heard a sharp crack of thunder and imagined the bed shook with the reverberations.

After a time, his breathing slowed and he rolled to his side, taking her with him. Their bodies entwined, his heart slowed and his breathing returned to normal as a sense of wellbeing crept in.

He'd fulfilled his duty.

Chapter Seven

Dani's gaze moved over Haaken as they lay together. His magnificent body was illuminated by the colored panes overhead and the brilliant moonlight that poured through them. Fully clothed he was a big man and his size hardly diminished with the absence of garments.

His chest was broad and well-defined by long hours spent practicing with a sword. Not an ounce of fat disrupted the long lean lines of his body. A pale yellow pane illuminated a thigh made muscular by hours in the saddle. Against her stomach, she could feel the heat of his semi-hard member and a quiver of womanly awareness clenched her sex.

As a virgin, she'd heard sex was a painful, messy occurrence and she'd grown up believing such. She'd secretly figured it couldn't be that bad as women allowed men to crawl between their thighs, nay, even encouraged it at times. After barely a week at the castle, she'd learned just how right she was as the women made use of the jaJin frequently.

Just as she would like to make use of Haaken again. Soon.

He lay quietly beside her, but she knew he did not sleep. His big hand was lazily stroking her back and she longed to stretch and purr like a cat. Her body still tingled from his possession and she wondered how long it would be before he would take her again.

"What are you thinking?"

Her face burned. There was no way she could tell him, even with the intimacies they'd shared. She tipped her head back to gaze at the upside-down stained glass window. "Tell me the story of the window."

Haaken's magical touch paused for a split second before he released her and rolled away. Suddenly chilled, she grabbed the silken sheet and began to pull it up to her chin.

"Don't." He towered over the bed. "I like looking at you."

Flustered, she arranged the pillows behind her, but made no move to cover herself.

Haaken gave her a warm look, then poured two glasses of Elyrian wine. "The window depicts a myth surrounding the house of Wryven. It is said that hundreds of years ago, Rik, the seventh count of Wryven, was a cruel man who pillaged and plundered the area to increase his holdings." He handed her a glass before retreating to a chair near the fire. "He raided villages, burned them to the ground and forced their inhabitants to swear loyalty to him and him alone.

"After one particular raid, a wise-woman was rousted from her house and he ordered it burned to the ground. It's said that she placed a curse upon him and his first-born son and every first-born son thereafter. Until the Wryven men found their one true mate and learned the importance of love, they would be cursed for all their days."

"What is the curse?" Dani took a sip of the pale green liquid, torn between wanting to savor the refreshing taste and hearing more of his tale.

"They'd turn into the form of the raven during the daylight hours. Only at night can they retain their male form."

"Has anyone ever broken the curse?"

"You don't doubt that there was a curse?" She heard the amusement in his voice.

"I've been on the road all of my life and I've seen many things I cannot explain. I once saw a man who drank blood and only came out at night because the sun burned his skin. I've heard stories of shapeshifters from all corners of the world. I heard one story of a man who could change into a cat at will, while another was forced to change with the cycles of the moon." She shrugged. "There's a great deal we don't understand about magic."

Haaken's expression was remote, his wine untouched as he stared at the towering window. There was a disturbing undercurrent as if something dark waited in the shadows with its breath drawn.

Dani shivered and put the glass aside.

"The curse has existed for centuries." He downed the contents of his glass in one swallow before he rose and stalked to the bed. The flickering fire illuminated his lean lines and bulging muscles. "The Wryven men married, bred and ruled with an iron fist and yet the curse still existed. Only at night were they in their human form, during the daylight, they were cursed to the form of the raven." He climbed on the bed and loomed over her, his big body dwarfing hers.

She leaned back into the pillows. "I don't see any feathers on you." She sounded breathless.

"Mmm..." He dipped his head and bit the sensitive area where her neck and shoulder joined, sending a jolt of anticipation through her. "Have you looked?"

"Umm," Dani fought to keep her eyes from rolling back in her head as he palmed her breast, his calloused thumb teasing her nipple, "I t-t-hink so."

"You might have missed a spot." His breath was hot against her skin. "Or maybe I missed one."

He lowered his head, his tongue dampening her nipples as his restless hands explored her hips and thighs. Dani curled her fingers in his long dark hair as he continued to lave her breasts. His mouth burned a trail of desire over her abdomen. He licked her hip as his big hand covered her woman's mound. Nudging her thighs with his hand, she parted them as he continued his lazy exploration of her body with his teeth and tongue.

She closed her eyes in the anticipation of his entry—that long, slow agonized rush of desire that lingered just out of reach. Instead of his entry, he continued his mind-bending exploration, finding places of pleasure she'd never dreamed existed. She released her grip on his hair as he nibbled the sensitive flesh of her inner thigh before breaching her damp core.

She arched, her breath sucked deep as he slid first one finger then another into her body, moving them in and out with silky ease.

"You're so wet for me," he breathed.

Dani forced her eyes open to the sight of Haaken between her thighs. His thumb stroked her nerve center and her hips arched, following his movement. His dark eyes glittered feverishly as he continued working her flesh with bold strokes and the fire spiraled higher. She dropped her head against the pillow and cried out as release washed over her body.

Before she could gather her scattered senses, Haaken withdrew his fingers and lowered his head to her sensitized flesh. At the first brush of his hot wet tongue, her eyes flew open and she gave a startled yelp.

The sight of his dark head between her thighs tightened her stomach as nature took over and she thrust against his mouth. One finger entered her slippery soft channel and began stroking as his tongue continued tantalizing. She thrashed against the pillows and Haaken grabbed her hips, holding her in place as he commanded her flesh. Her body arched higher as tension grew and her nerves sang with arousal.

"Come for me."

His voice rumbled against her flesh and tumbled her over the edge. White-hot stars burst forth as she shattered into a million pieces. Dani fell limp against the bed, her pile of pillows now scattered. Sated, she licked her lips, knowing she couldn't move if she tried. She could feel him moving, the bed shifting beneath his weight. He spread her thighs and pressed her knees toward her breasts. She felt the insistent press of his erection against her mound.

"Look at me," he growled. "I want to see your eyes as I consume you."

Dani forced her eyes open as Haaken plunged into her with a force that left them both breathless. She stretched beneath him, raising her ankles to link around his waist, forcing him deeper. Her nails dug into his back as she met him stroke for stroke, heated flesh slapped against heated flesh as they gave as good as they received.

As promised, he consumed her. Her world receded to the bed and his pounding cock and hot mouth as he feasted on her flesh, bringing her to completion so many times she lost count. She couldn't have been more branded than if he'd burned his name into her skin. He mumbled words in a language she didn't recognize as he thrust into her. It was lyrical, almost a chant, and she lost herself in the cadence of his words and magical possession.

His movements quickened, his pelvis thundered against her. Suddenly his muscles tensed as his magnificent head was thrown back and he shouted his fulfillment. Dani wrapped her arms around his shoulders as he collapsed into her. She closed her eyes, savoring the feel of him still buried deep within her.

"Well?"

Haaken scowled at Ty before returning his gaze to the ripening sky. "Well, what?"

"Was she any good?" Ty refilled his glass of Elyrian wine. "I took KayLe and Mara to bed and they fucked my brains out. I'm surprised I could get out of bed to meet with you."

Haaken ignored his brother, preferring to concentrate on the coming sunrise. Had his mating with Dani succeeded in breaking the curse or would the sunrise send him into raven form once more?

"You aren't answering me," Ty said.

"Nor will I," Haaken grunted. He took the glass from Ty's hand and drained it before handing it back.

"What's the problem?" Ty refilled the glass. "We've shared women before and you've never shied from the details before now." He set down the decanter with a clang. "She's really *the One*, isn't she?"

Haaken scowled as his brother stared at him, a comically shocked expression on his face. "For the love of Ola, what are you talking about?"

"You're in love with her."

"I'm nothing of the sort—"

"Then you're falling in love with her." Ty shook his head, his expression amused. "Who would have thought I'd see the day my brother fell in love with a commoner, a little slave girl at that."

"You're a fool. I'm not in love with her nor will I fall in love with her. She's my fated one, the one to break the curse. I'll fuck her until she reaches completion many times over, she'll give me children and she'll want for nothing for the rest of her life so this curse can be broken." He reached for the glass. "No more no less."

Ty chuckled and raised the glass in a mock salute. "I think you protest too strongly here, my brother. It's almost as if you seek to convince yourself of this."

Panic fluttered in his chest and Haaken turned away to stare outside again. He couldn't be in love with Dani, he couldn't. Wryven men were cursed with horrendous luck with women and, if they were foolish enough to fall in love with them, it was a sure death for the unlucky woman. Many Wryven wives had died in childbirth or by a pernicious fever that would overtake a seemingly healthy woman, reducing her to a shriveled corpse in mere weeks.

True, he was the first Wryven male to find the woman who was marked as told in the lore of the myth. But could Dani survive the curse? His fist clenched. It was too much to risk. She was but a means to an end and that was the only way he could allow himself to view her.

On the horizon, the sun continued its inexorable climb. As it breached the horizon, Haaken felt the familiar tingling sensation that heralded his transformation. "It didn't work. Why didn't it work?"

"She's marked," Ty said. He dropped the glass and it shattered on the stone floor. "How could it have not worked?" He opened the window of the tower room and the cool morning breeze swirled in.

"She's the One, I feel it." Haaken shot an agonized look at his brother as sparks flew from his fingertips and golden light consumed his body. He shook his head. "I know not—"

Light swirled about his head and his feet left the ground as the transformation continued. As the world receded around him, he heard Ty speak.

"You'd better find out brother, you're running out of time."

Chapter Eight

Dani slipped from her room, hoping no one had seen her leave Haaken's rooms earlier in the same clothes she had worn last night. She'd been disappointed to awaken alone, only the scent of him upon her skin to convince her that the events of last night had really occurred.

She couldn't prevent a smile as she made her way down the hall. Her body ached in places she'd never dreamed even existed. Haaken was a masterful lover and she could hardly wait to see what the evening held in store for them.

The sun was high as she made her way through one of the many courtyards, a short cut to the kitchens. She would grab something to break her fast, then find Ren to see how her evening had gone.

The castle was curiously quiet, no doubt due to the late hours from the festivities of last evening. But she heard the clang of steel against steel of the warriors engaged in swordplay in the outer bailey.

She slipped into the cavernous kitchens, and the scent of roasting meat and freshly baked bread caused her stomach to growl. Two kitchen maids sat on low stools, sorting through a large basket of greens, and Dani gave them a shy smile as she passed. The cooks were nowhere to be seen but their morning's work was evident. Fresh fruit and vegetables were laid across the central table awaiting preparation for the evening meal. Dani selected a small round tropiel and a few grapes.

Another table near the ovens was piled high with golden loaves of bread, crisp crackers and fruity tarts. Spying the lemon ones, Dani took one to add to her bounty.

Biting into the flaky tart, she could barely contain her groan of delight as the fresh lemon flavor swamped her senses. In the hall, she heard voices approaching the kitchens. Not wishing to see anyone, she grabbed a small square of cheese and escaped into the courtyard.

Beneath one of the kitchen windows, she spied a small private bench tucked behind a potted tree. After arranging her meal in her lap, she settled in to enjoy the air and her food.

"She's fresh meat, that's why he wanted her."

Dani tensed when she recognized KayLe's voice coming from the kitchens.

"I think you're jealous."

She didn't recognize the second voice.

"Me, jealous of that skinny little *traveler*?" KayLe snorted. "I don't think so. Haaken will soon lose interest in her and return to my bed where he belongs."

"But the Tuli-tay was held last night—"

"That makes no difference. He will still return to me." There was no mistaking the anger in her voice. "He must fulfill his obligation to his people, but he doesn't have to remain faithful to the little creature. Wryven men have very healthy...appetites. A half-starved little scarecrow won't be able to keep a man like Haaken satisfied very long." Dani heard the agitated rattle of silverware. "She's simply a new fascination and all that means is I'll have to work doubly hard to ensure that he returns to me. The sooner the better."

"What about her?"

"What about her? He'll lock her up in a remote location and he and I can get back to life as usual." KayLe gave a sultry laugh. "All will be as it should."

A drawer slammed shut and the voices faded. Dani slumped against the wall, a bite of lemon tart wedged in her throat. Was KayLe right? Would Haaken grow tired of her and lock her away somewhere? He still believed she was a slave—his slave—and she'd made no attempt to disabuse him of the notion.

She tossed the rest of the tart at the base of the potted tree. She needed to get out of here. She tucked the fruit and cheese in her pocket and headed for the door leading to her wing. In the distance, she heard a shout, then the distant clang of a bell. Thanks to the high walls of the keep, the sounds were muffled and distorted. Then a door flew open and Ren ran into the courtyard. There was no mistaking the panic on her face.

"Oh Dani, it's awful." Her feet barely touched the walk. "The village is on fire."

"On fire? Where?"

"In the poorer section where they have thatched roofs. Haaken wanted to get rid of them, said they were too hazardous—"

"How many homes?" Dani grabbed Ren to stop her flood of words. "How many homes are at stake?"

"Dozens—" Her voice broke with a sob.

Dani grabbed her hand and pulled her toward the kitchens. The maids who'd been working on the greens were up and leaning out the window, yelling at someone.

"You." Dani grabbed a blonde-haired girl. "Round up some people to gather blankets and bed linens. We need as much as we can find. Raid the stores, do whatever you have to do, but get them."

The girl bit her lip then nodded, scurrying off to do as she was bid.

Dani pointed to the dark-haired one. "You, get some women and find some cloth to be used for bandages. Cut them and bring them to the town, we'll need them."

She nodded and ran off in the wake of the other maid.

"What do you want me to do?" Ren asked.

"Find the healers, all of them, and direct them to the site. We'll need lots of help."

Ren nodded. "And what will you do?"

"I'm going down there to see how I can help."

"Be careful," Ren said.

Dani gave her a quick hug and ushered her on her way. Pausing only to grab all the available toweling from the kitchen closet, she loaded her arms and took off at a dead run. As she burst into the outer bailey, Mik approached.

"Where do you think you're going?"

"To help."

He shook his head. "I've got my orders and you're not to leave the keep."

Dani scowled at him. Even as young as he was, he was twice her size and she would undoubtedly lose in a physical confrontation. "And I have to help. Either help me or get out of my way."

"You cannot leave—"

"I can and I will." She shoved the armload of cloth at the warrior and, judging from his startled expression, it was the last thing he'd expected her to do. "People are *dying* down there.

Either help me help them or by Ola, I'll go through you to get there."

She wheeled away and charged through the gates, praying no one made any attempt to stop her. The road to town led directly to the square. At this distance, she could see the fire was to the east and it would be faster to leave the road and run through the fields to get there.

Gathering her skirts, she dashed through the thick grass, her heart pounding and her mouth dry with fear. From this distance, she could see the billowing black clouds of smoke and leaping flames as the homes were consumed.

Behind her she heard the thud of hooves and she saw Mik and another man each astride a horse. The second man's arms were stuffed with towels. "I cannot let you go alone," Mik said. He held out his hand and, without thinking twice, Dani grabbed it and was pulled up behind him.

"Thank you."

He gave a curt nod and kicked the horse into a run. Within moments, they entered the melee. Dozens of farmers and their families were milling in the streets. Haaken's warriors were trying to direct them to safety by forcing them to exit the area while other warriors and farmers had formed a bucket line and were trying to save the thatched houses still standing.

Dani slid from the horse and grabbed the arm of the nearest lieutenant. "Where are the wounded being taken?"

He gave her a startled look, then nodded at the towering church a few blocks west. "There. We're taking them there."

She nodded her thanks and grabbed the towels from Mik's companion. She ran, leaving them to follow or join the bucket line.

The air had a sooty, smoky scent and she forced herself to breathe through her mouth as she approached the church.

Already they were full to capacity and bodies lay outside the stone walls as well. Some moved, crying in pain, while others were ominously still.

Her heart breaking, she was glad to see Mik behind her. "I need water, as much as you can carry," she said to him. "And any medical supplies you can find."

The man gave her a quick nod and vanished into the milling crowd. Swallowing her fear, she waded into the mass of injured and dying. Soon she was cleaning wounds, applying bandages and holding hands as the seriously injured crossed into the netherworld of Ola, the creator.

As she worked, smoke swallowed the sun. At one point, Dani looked up to see Ren nearby as she held a dying woman's hand. The woman's hair had been burned away and her skin was horribly blistered.

Other women and a few men worked alongside them. There were several healers with their salves and potions, but all too soon their supplies were depleted and they were forced to use common drinking ale to bathe injuries before wrapping them in clean linen. Priests issued comfort as they moved among the injured, their heads bowed and their robes stained with blood and soot, their lips issuing prayer after prayer as they worked.

How many hours passed she didn't know as she toiled among the sick and dying. Her body ached from constant stooping and bending, but she refused to stop. They needed her.

As darkness descended, she heard a murmur through the crowd that the flames had been conquered. Giving a quick prayer of thanks, she bent her head to hear the dying prayers of a young woman, her lifeless child still in her arms. Eyes burning, Dani smoothed the woman's scorched hair from her forehead as her breathing grew more ragged. Finally, she drew her last breath and her body relaxed into death.

Dani sat back, her neck aching and her heart sore. So many had died here today, so many lives lost and homes destroyed. Across the churchyard, Ren stood near the church door in the arms of her lover. The massive warrior held her as she sobbed. He swung her into his arms and bore her off into the darkness.

Around her, victims lay bundled in blankets, their injuries swathed in white linen. The dead had been transported to an area outside of town where a group of warriors dug the graves.

Dani rose and motioned for the men to come and collect the woman and her child. Her heart was numb as they wrapped the tiny body in a linen shroud before wrapping the mother and child together then carrying them off into the darkness.

Down the street, she saw KayLe. The woman had arrived an hour before with a cartload of food that Dani had ordered for the men. The hungry warriors lined up and were receiving portions of roasted meat and bread with KayLe their charming hostess. Every hair in place, her skin no doubt perfumed and her clothing immaculate, the woman laughed and flirted with the exhausted, filthy men.

Dani turned away. At least KayLe was doing something useful for the first time today. She was too tired to even feel resentment toward the woman, there was too much to do.

One of the women gestured to her and Dani gathered her meager supplies. She was administering to a child with a cut on her leg when she heard a commotion near the food wagon. She looked up to see the Overseer join a group of his warriors. Her heart quickened at the sight of her lover, hearty and hale. Behind him was a large number of his personal guard. He disbursed them to give aid before scanning the crowds.

KayLe, who was in the process of handing out bread, thrust the loaf toward a small hunched farmer before flinging herself into Haaken's arms. Even from a distance, Dani could see she was sobbing wildly. Numb, Dani turned away to tuck a blanket around the now-sleeping girl. Her face was dirty with soot and her blonde curls were dulled, but she still looked like a sleeping angel.

She rose and placed her hands at her waist to stretch her back when a wave of dizziness assailed her and she stumbled, placing her hands on the church wall to regain her balance. She was at the end of her strength and needed to rest. Maybe she could send one of the other women for something to drink. She groped for the bench she knew was nearby when her fingers encountered warm leather.

She looked up into Haaken's dark face as her knees wobbled. His arms slid around her waist and he pulled her into the sanctuary of his arms. Dani closed her eyes and inhaled the scent of clean man and leather. She knew she looked a sight but she couldn't bring herself to care now that his arms were around her.

"Thank you for taking care of my people," he said.

She nodded, too numb to respond verbally. Her hands fisted in the front of his vest.

"Come, I'll take you back to the keep where you can rest."

"I need to—"

"No, you've done enough for today. You need to rest as there'll be a great deal to do in the morning as well."

Exhausted beyond comprehension, Dani clung to him as Haaken steered her through the churchyard. As they reached the street, his squire appeared leading his stallion. Haaken swung onto the horse and, with the squire's help, Dani was settled before him.

She sagged against him, her eyes drifting closed as the sounds of the village faded and darkness embraced them. She slid her fingers between the laces on his shirt, needing to feel his skin, warm and alive, beneath her fingertips. She closed her eyes and felt a fleeting caress on her hair as she welcomed the darkness, knowing for the moment that Haaken would take care of everything.

She didn't stir when he laid her on the bed. She'd fallen asleep in his arms on the back of a horse. A testament to her exhaustion.

Haaken moved to the attached bathing chamber. All extraneous personnel had been dispatched to the village to assist the victims, leaving Dani's care in his hands. From a spout on the wall, he set the spring-hot water to flowing into the marble tub.

Once the bath was filled, he went back into the bedchamber. Moonlight poured through the colored panes of the window, illuminating the woman who'd managed to work her way into his world and, with her selfless actions today, his heart.

Haaken stared down at her. She'd done more than he could have expected. The Wryven weren't her people. As a traveler, they'd have shunned both her and her family, yet she'd organized the household to come to the rescue. He wouldn't have blamed her if she hadn't lifted a finger to help but she did, and she'd saved lives.

After removing her ruined clothing, he checked for injuries. Other than being covered in soot, she appeared to be unharmed. He scooped her into his arms, then carried her into the bathroom. She made a soft murmur and her eyelashes flickered, but she didn't awaken as he settled her in the low seat in the tub. He shucked everything but his loincloth and climbed in with her. As he raised her leg and began soaping her skin, her eyes opened.

Her smile was slow, sensual as he ran the suds-laden cloth up her calf then down again. Her anklet sang out as he brushed the little bells with the cloth.

"My jaJin." Her voice was slurred with exhaustion.

"That's right." He kissed the inside of her knee. "Now lie back and relax while I see to your every need."

Dani settled into the tub as he picked up her other leg and she giggled as he took great care to wash between each toe. He skimmed his hands up and down her thighs, careful to not touch her soft womanly core other than several quick swipes with the cloth. She moaned in protest as he moved away and Haaken felt a quick jolt of satisfaction. Even exhausted, she was completely responsive to his touch.

He moved between her knees as he worked up her body. He soaped her arms, taking great care to massage the knots out of her shoulders placed there by her exhausting work. Then he discarded the cloth and soaped his hands before running them over her breasts, her nipples pebbling against his palms. Her hips shifted restlessly in the water.

Her eyes opened, slumberous. "I want you."

He shook his head though his cock was telling him something else entirely. "You need to rest, Dani. For a few hours at least."

"But—"

"Shh." He brushed his finger over her lips, stilling her words.

Haaken retrieved the cloth and rinsed it before running it over her face. Soft winged brows, dark blonde lashes that shadowed her pale cheeks, her pert little nose and her luscious mouth—

His hips lunged forward as her talented fingers found his cock through the wet loincloth. Her eyes opened and he tumbled headlong into their velvet depths.

"You want me," she whispered.

"More than life itself," he said.

"Then why do you hesitate?" She released him and fumbled with the sodden material of his loincloth. "I want to feel you inside me."

Why was he hesitating? Was it because he'd seen a different side to this enchanting woman? Because she was much more than just a means to an end for him and his family?

"Dani—"

The loincloth fell away and she wrapped her hands around his cock, halting his words. Regardless of what his mind was telling him, his body needed her badly and, with her actions, there was no doubt in his mind what Dani wanted.

Allowing her to take the lead, he braced his hands on the edge of the tub on either side of her head. A hiss slipped through his teeth as she gently squeezed his cock before directing him to her womanly core. As he brushed her soft folds, he gave a strangled cry.

"Dani." He lunged forward, burying his cock in her depths as he took her mouth with a fury he'd rarely ever displayed with a woman. Heat, lust and the desire for possession rose hot in his blood as their tongues teased and tempted.

Her hips arched, forcing him deeper. Unable to help himself, he drove into her, her wild cry muffled by his marauding mouth. Her knees tightened around his hips as he took her, deep, hard. Water sloshed over the edge of the tub as he pounded into her, each movement causing the tension to spiral higher.

His entire body burned, her every touch electrified his nerves. Vaguely he was aware of her cries as she tightened around him when a flood of sensation crested, obliterating everything else as his body gained the release he so desperately craved.

Dani awakened slowly, aware of the weight of a hairy male arm tossed over her abdomen, pinning her to the bed. Turning her head, she saw Haaken stretched beside her, his magnificent body bathed in flickering firelight.

He lay on his stomach; the sheets were tangled around his ankles where he'd kicked them off. Haaken in full garb was impressive; in the raw, he was mouth-watering.

His long legs were straight and muscular, sprinkled with black hair. His buttocks were firm and rounded, his waist narrow before widening into broad, muscular shoulders. His arm, roped with toned flesh and sinew, was tossed over her waist. His forearm was heavy and she lightly ran her hand across it, relishing the warmth and tensile strength of her lover in repose.

His hand was splayed on her side. She rubbed her fingers over his, noting the numerous scars from his hard-won life. As protector of the province, his was a hard life of constant negotiations for peace and, when it came down to it, war.

A woman would be a fool to hand her heart to such a man.

She held her breath as she removed his arm from her body. He made a sound in his sleep and his hips shifted restlessly before he stilled.

So, she was a fool.

Dani rose and sat on her heels, looking at him. He'd stolen her heart with barely a word. It was his actions, his friendly yet commanding interaction with his men, his tolerance and patience with the villagers and his desire to aid them in gaining a better life that demonstrated more about his character than any words he could speak.

And there was no way she could repay him for saving her from her former life. He'd given her more than she'd ever dreamed and she yearned for a way to say thank you.

Dani leaned forward and pressed a kiss to the indentation of his spine. She smiled as he twitched beneath her touch. She moved lower, kissing and licking a path over the plump curve of his buttock before she bit him.

"Hey!" His head popped out of the pillows.

She laughed and patted him on one firm cheek, then squeezed. Taking her other hand, she gave his other cheek the same treatment.

"I'm not a melon, woman," he growled. "What do you think you're doing?"

"Mmm." She gave him one final pat. "Checking out my merchandise." He started to roll and she stopped him by straddling his narrow hips. She leaned forward, pressing her breasts into his back and forcing him back against the bed. "Not yet, my jaJin. I'm still checking."

Haaken's dark chuckle turned to a choke as she shimmied down his body. The sensation of his bronzed skin against her erect nipples caused a rush of warmth between her thighs. Then his muscles tightened as she stroked upward.

"Do you like that?" Her voice was husky and she barely recognized it as her own.

He made a soft growl as his fingers clenched the bedding.

"Shall I be softer?" She rose so that her nipples barely brushed his flesh and she could feel him shudder beneath her touch. "Harder?" She pressed down, flattening her upper body against his back. "Or maybe none at all?" She rose, her body aching with the need to be fulfilled, but enjoying the game too much to rush.

She squealed when he twisted beneath her. She pitched sideways, but he grabbed her before she could fall off the bed and settled her over him, his cock warm and hard against the damp notch of her thighs.

With a self-satisfied smile, Haaken reclined against the pillows, his arms raised with his hands behind his head.

"As your jaJin, it would behoove me to inform you that you've only inspected half of your merchandise. I would hate to think that you'd select me for your pleasure, then be...disappointed."

As if that could happen.

Dani leaned forward, anticipation moving through her nervous system. "How right you are, jaJin."

He shifted so she could kiss him, but she avoided his handsome mouth, opting instead to kiss his throat. His chest was warm beneath her hand and she could feel his accelerated heartbeat. He may act unmoved, but the growing hardness pressing against her and his deepening breaths told another story completely.

She nibbled a path down his body, pausing to lick a spot or bite a nipple. She arched against him, reveling in the feel of his throbbing cock against her sensitive opening.

But she wanted more, much more.

She stretched and reached for a small bottle of massage oil on the bedside table. As she uncorked it, the rich scent of aloinnin blossoms rose from the pale oil. Aloinnin, a powerful nerve enhancer, was coveted among lovers young and old.

Aware of his dark gaze, she moved so that his cock sprang free between them. Pouring oil on her hands, she shuddered as she coated his stiff rod with the fragrant liquid. When his skin was glistening and Haaken was panting, she released him.

"jaJin, I want you to pleasure yourself." She moved back until she was settled between his feet against the footboard. Her legs spread, her feet framing his hips, she rubbed the excess oil into her thighs. "I want to watch."

Haaken's gaze was fixed on her spread legs and the damp flesh between them. He licked his lips as he reached for his cock. His big fingers encircled and he began to stroke. Slow at first, concentrating on prolonging the sensation as he worked his hand over his straining flesh.

Dani continued rubbing oil into her skin when what she really wanted was either to touch herself or launch herself at the cock being prepared before her very eyes.

She slid a finger into her dampened folds, lightly grazing her bundle of nerves. The aloinnin oil caused a rush of heat so sharp it bordered on pain. She moaned and repeated her movement, her body arching against her hand.

"I need to touch you."

Dani opened her eyes to see Haaken, his face straining, his cock bulging from his fist. He looked as if he, too, were in pain.

"My poor jaJin," she said. She moved to her knees, brushing his hands away, her fingers barely encircling his wrists. She leaned over, imprisoning his hands against the bed while his cock nestled deep between her thighs where it belonged. "Let me help you."

She spread her legs, her knees rubbing the outside of his hips as she rocked against him, knowing the heat of the oil and the incredible size and hardness of him would quickly take her over the edge. She rotated her hips, slowly at first then increasing the pressure as the tension mounted.

She couldn't stop a long, loud groan of release as a tidal wave of sensation washed through her. Spasms continued to shake her for several moments even after she'd collapsed on his chest.

"Do I please you, mistress?"

She sighed. "Yes, my jaJin, you please me greatly."

"Good."

Then, without warning, Haaken stretched one arm over her head taking her wrists with him. Then, he looped his arm around her waist, then rolled over and buried himself in her again with one smooth movement.

Dani gave a strangled cry as he loomed, filling her, overpowering her. She looped her legs around his waist as he pounded—stretching and filling her beyond belief. The sensation of this man inside her was one she longed to savor, but not this time, the fever was too intense.

Her consciousness faded to this man, this room, as he took her to the heights of ecstasy, again and again. Just when she thought she could bear no more and she was on the verge of begging him to stop, he'd reach down and stroke her with one broad finger until she soared again.

With the big bed shuddering beneath them, Haaken roared his completion, his body straining and jerking with the force of his release. Dani gloried in the beauty of this man who'd possessed her, his face damp with sweat, his eyes closed, focused on his pleasure.

He collapsed over her and she reveled in the weight and heat of his big body. She slid her arms around his shoulders, her fingers tangling in his damp hair as she closed her eyes. She couldn't ask for anything more.

Chapter Nine

"What do you mean I can't leave?" Dani hugged the newly cut bundle of bandages to her chest.

"The Overseer gave his orders. You're not to leave the keep." Mik shut the door she'd just opened only, this time, he hung a padlock on the heavy iron hasp effectively locking her in the keep. "If you need anything, it will be brought to you."

"How can I help the villagers if I can't go down there?" Tears of frustration stung her eyes. "I can't do anything from here."

"I'm sorry, but I have my orders." He looked decidedly uncomfortable at the sight of her tears.

"So you said." Dani blindly shoved the bundle at him and stalked back to the castle.

Nothing had changed between her and Haaken. Nothing at all. He still sought to keep her as a slave and not allow her any say in her life. Which meant she couldn't stay here any longer. He didn't love her and she wouldn't remain here without his declaration of love. If he did, he'd never have ordered her to be locked in the keep. How was he any different than her father? She had more food than she could eat and clothes to rival any woman's closet, but a cage was a cage no matter how gilded the bars.

Haaken's bedchamber was empty and she slammed the door behind her. The room had been set to rights, the linens on the massive bed had been changed, the fireplace cleaned and a fresh fire laid, waiting only for the touch of a flame to set it alight.

Just like her.

She sank to her knees in the midst of the woven silk carpet. Her head bowed, she allowed the tears to come. Softly at first, the trickle turned into a torrent as she contemplated her uncertain future with a man who neither trusted nor respected her. Haaken had changed the scenery and released her from her chain, but, with Mik's orders this morning, it was apparent that nothing had changed at all.

What kind of future was that?

Dani stared overhead at the soaring stained glass windows. The Wryven curse might be true for it seemed the Wryven men didn't understand that love wasn't about imprisonment and keeping someone at arm's length. Love was about risk, the risk of losing one's heart to another. Love was about trust, trusting one's mate to be faithful and do nothing to harm anyone including themselves. Love was about joy, the sheer joy of being alive and in love. The sense of belonging it brought.

But Haaken wouldn't know any of that.

Which meant she couldn't stay here any longer. Her eyes closed against the pain at the thought of leaving. She'd exchanged one cage for another. She couldn't go back to her family and she couldn't stay with Haaken viewing her as a possession rather than his mate. His lover. His equal.

She dried her face with the sleeve of her dress. She'd accept no less from any man, especially the love of her life. Dani struggled to her feet, knowing each step drove home the wedge that Haaken had begun with his careless orders.

Haaken ran down the steps from the tower room. The sun had set and he'd received an update from Ty as to the casualties in the village and the extent of the rebuilding efforts. But, as Ty had droned on, all he could think about was Dani. He was still puzzled by his lack of transformation into a complete human. If she was the one and she was marked as foretold in the legend, why was he still consigned to the form of the raven during daylight hours? He'd taken Dani as his mate and given her everything she desired. What more could he do to break the curse?

The house was curiously still, the air heavy as if its inhabitants awaited some event to put it into action. Nothing looked amiss, but there was something wrong. He couldn't quite put his finger on what was different but something just didn't feel right.

The door to his bedchamber stood open and empty when he entered. Where was she? He headed for the main staircase. He hoped she wasn't too mad at him for putting a halt to her excursions, but the countryside outside the castle walls was too dangerous to let her run free. If his enemies deduced who she was, there was no telling what could happen to her. Above all, he had to keep her safe for both their sakes.

He reached the main floor and started for the entrance when the sound of someone crying stopped him. He frowned and followed the sound to the solarium.

Dani sat on the rim of a small fountain, her face pale and composed. Dressed in pale pink silk, she'd never looked more beautiful or remote. Beside her sat Ren, her face blotchy as tears streamed down her cheeks. Had Lorn done something to hurt his sister? If he had, Haaken would tear the man limb from limb.

As he entered the room, Dani's gaze shifted from his sister to him. Her cool expression didn't alter when her eyes met his and a chill of foreboding ran down his spine.

"Ren?" He stopped a few feet away from the women. "What's wrong?"

Dani removed her hand from Ren's shoulder as his sister rose. She gave her brother a sad shrug before ducking around him and running from the room.

"Dani?"

"I love you." She sat straight and tall, her expression remote.

Haaken forced a slight smile against the growing sense of impending doom. "You don't sound happy about it."

"You're wrong. I'm very happy about loving you, but I can't live here any longer." She gestured toward a small bag near the door. "I'm leaving. Tonight."

Leaving? A sense of unreality washed over him. In one breath, she'd said she loved him and in the next, she'd announced she was leaving. How could she leave?

She shook her head. "You don't love me, you desire me. I thought that might be enough, but it isn't. After yesterday and what I saw in the village, I realize it isn't enough. Not anymore. I want it all, Haaken. I want more than your body. I need all of you and you cannot give me what I need."

"You're talking foolishness, woman." He clenched his fist. "I'll not allow it."

"Yes, you will." She rose from her perch. "If you don't, you'll risk my love turning to hate. Is that what you want? For me to hate you?"

He scowled. Of course he didn't want her to hate him, but the words stuck in his throat.

She stepped closer and her scent wrapped around his senses. Her gaze was searching and he fought the urge to turn away. Never had he run from a challenge, so why did he want to turn away from this small woman?

"You can't even say it, can you?" Her voice was sad.

"By Ola, what do you want from me, woman?"

She stepped back. "You know what I want. Only you can decide how much I really mean to you." She picked up the bag and walked away, her back straight and shoulders squared. The tiny bells on her ankle chimed as she moved toward the door.

Haaken followed, his steps slow. He didn't want her to leave, but he couldn't give her what she asked. To offer his heart would spell their doom as it had for his ancestors.

Haven't you already lost your heart to her?

He ignored the taunting voice in his head. Yes, he had and look what that had gotten him. She was leaving anyway.

But you haven't told her.

Why should he? She'd still leave and have the satisfaction of knowing she'd stolen his heart as well. No, he wouldn't do it.

The outer bailey was bustling with warriors and staff going about their duties before bedding down for the night. As Dani made her way to the gate, their activities stopped and people watched her slim form. Most, if not all, of the inhabitants of the keep were aware of his restrictions upon her movements and they were curious as to her business.

The head gatekeeper approached, holding out his hand to stop her progress. They stood together for a few moments, then he looked up at Haaken in the doorway.

For a second, the only sound was that of a squalling child. Even the wind seemed halted as everyone waited to see what he'd do. As he stood there, more and more eyes moved between

Dani and him. She stood facing toward the gate, her posture tense as if expecting him to refuse her.

He motioned to Mik. "Follow her. See that no harm comes to her but don't aid her, in any other manner."

"Yes, sire." The warrior walked down the steps toward Dani.

Haaken nodded to the gatekeeper then turned away, not wanting to see her leave. Dani would return to him.

She must.

Chapter Ten

Four moon cycles later

Ren threw open the door of his study and stomped in. One look at her face told Haaken that his baby sister had reached the end of her patience. "When are you going after her?"

"Not now, Ren." Haaken dismissed her and returned to the documents on his desk. He had work to accomplish in the next few hours and he couldn't afford any more distractions.

She reached over and snatched the papers off the top of the desk. "Yes, now!"

Haaken rose. "I don't have time for this—"

"Make time." She held the papers just out of his reach.

"I am your Overseer—"

"You're my brother first!" She dropped her arm. "Or have you forgotten already?"

Ty came running into the room, sword drawn, with several guards behind him. He slid to a halt, his gaze moving as he looked for signs of trouble. "What's all the yelling about?" He slipped the sword back into his scabbard before catching Ren's braid and tugging her close for a ferocious hug.

Haaken cringed as his financial reports were crushed between his siblings. Was nothing sacred?

"Haaken is being unreasonable." Ren's voice was muffled against the front of Ty's vest.

"There's a switch." He released his sister and waved the guards out of the room. "Usually you're the one being unreasonable."

Ren scowled at her brother, then stomped to a chair and dropped into it in a flurry of yellow silk. "You're never on my side," she grumbled.

Haaken barely controlled his annoyance as he watched her crease the pages even further.

"What did he do now?" Ty asked.

"He won't go get her." She riffled the crumpled sheets in an attempt to put them back in order. "I'm getting married in a fortnight and Dani won't be there because of *him*."

"Ah." The one word held a wealth of meaning in its utterance.

"What does that mean?" Haaken stomped around his desk and snatched the papers from Ren's destructive fingertips. "This isn't any of your business."

"Actually, this concerns all of us *and* our progeny." Ty moved to the side table where a variety of wines sat available for guests. Invited guests, unlike his siblings. "The reality of our situation is that you're still cursed and time is marching on." He offered a glass of Elyrian wine to Ren, then sat with his own drink. "We need to talk about the future of this family."

Haaken smoothed the pages on his desk. Since Dani had left the keep, he'd avoided this subject altogether. They were all aware that, the older he grew, the more hours he was forced to remain in raven form. And, as his thirtieth year approached, the time lost as a human became greater. Since she'd gone, he'd lost more than an hour and a half. Soon enough, he'd change into animal form and never return.

Haaken sat back, unutterably weary. He was tired of fighting the inevitable. He was tired of fighting with his sister and brother. Most of all he was tired of being haunted by Dani's ghost.

At night, as he tried to work on the myriad of details involved with running his lands, she'd invaded his senses and distracted him from his duties. He'd imagine a whiff of her perfume or her merry laugh or the tinkling of her ankle bells.

At first, he'd mistakenly believed that she'd returned. But every time he'd leapt from his chair to find no one but the ever-present guards in the hall.

Mik still kept a close eye on Dani. She'd rented a small house on the edge of the village where she did embroidery and mending. For the past four and a half moon cycles—not that he was counting—she'd managed to keep a roof over her head, food on the table and clothing on her back and he was proud of her accomplishments.

He'd seen her once at a distance on market day. He'd ventured into the village hoping to catch a glimpse of her. She'd been purchasing colored thread and looked better than ever. She'd added a few more pounds and her cheeks had glowed with good health. She'd been laughing with the merchant as she bartered for threads in exchange for embroidered handkerchiefs. After collecting her purchases, she'd left and he could have sworn he'd heard the tinkling of little bells.

"It's time you brought her home." Ren downed her wine in a single gulp and Haaken winced, knowing the kick the liquid would have on his little sister.

"I agree." Ty rose and retrieved the bottle. "We need Dani back. You need Dani back." He filled both Ren's and his glasses, then set the bottle on the floor between them. "It's right for all of us."

Haaken reached into a desk drawer and withdrew a flask of Darnarian liquor, the liquid bright blue against the clear glass. Since it looked like a drinking event, he'd best join in or be left behind. He took a swallow and the liquid burned a path of fire down his throat to pool warmly in his stomach.

"I've already fulfilled the instructions of the myth," he said. "And I'm still cursed. It's obvious to me that we were wrong. She's not the one."

"She is, I feel it." Ren leaned forward. "The curse states that, until the cursed one finds their true love and learns the importance of it, they're doomed to a half-life."

"We know that." Ty swirled the liquid in the glass. "What's your point, little sister?"

Ren gave him a narrow look. "Haaken found his true love." She rolled her eyes at Haaken. "Not that he'll admit it, though. The problem is he hasn't learned the important part. That's where he went wrong."

Ty frowned. "You might be onto something—"

"Of course I am. It's an integral part of the curse. It's more than simply having Dani in his life, the importance is about understanding what love means." Ren reached for the wine bottle.

"Sex," Ty said.

Ren rolled her eyes. "Ola, save me." She filled her glass. "Haaken, what do you think love is?"

He took another quick drink to give him time to avoid her question. What did he think love was? In his life, feelings of love had been few and far between. Yes, he loved his siblings no matter how much they annoyed him. But that love was different from the love between a man and women. Before Dani, he could honestly say he'd never been in love. Lust, yes; love, no. Did he desire her? Yes. He enjoyed her company and her laugh, and he missed having her beside him. But did that equate to love?

"I don't know," Haaken said.

Ren snorted in disgust. "You'd better figure it out soon, brother."

"Even if you don't figure out what the important part is," Ty said. "You're doomed to lose your humanity. Don't you think you should make your peace with her before it's too late?"

"I don't have anything to say—"

"Liar," Ren said.

Haaken glared at his sister, noticing the soft flush of alcohol on her skin.

"You have a lot to say to Dani, just admit it," Ty said.

Haaken drank deeply and with every swallow, the burn lessened and an odd restless, almost expectant feeling took hold. Could he go to her?

"Yeah, admit it." Ren stood, weaving slightly before she caught herself. "I'm leaving."

"Where are you going?" Ty asked.

"To find Lorn. I think I'll fuck his brains out." Ren swayed toward the door. "All this talk of love has made me...itchy."

Haaken winced at the thought of his sister and the warrior. While he'd granted them dispensation to marry, the knowledge of when they were indulging themselves was more than he wished to hear.

"So what will it be, brother?" Ty rose. "Will you go to her or end your mortal life with regrets?" He shook his head. "It would be a shame for Dani to never hear how you feel about her."

Haaken turned away and stared out the window into the darkness. Before him lay Wryven. The city and its people he'd been raised to lead and protect. What kind of a leader was he if he couldn't confront the woman who'd stolen his heart? He'd always thought his father to be a coward in his treatment of his mother, Lady Wyn. Now he'd done the exact same thing to Dani. He'd refused to tell her the truth and confront his demons.

He took another drink of the liquor. It would seem he really was his father's son after all.

There's still time...

Yes.

She loves you, you love her...

Dani belonged with him. By his side for however long he had left as a human. Midnight was approaching and, slowly but surely, the lights were being extinguished in Wryven. His brother was right, time was running out.

Chapter Eleven

The nights were the hardest.

Dani rolled in her narrow bed, her gown twisted about her hips. Overhead, the full moon peeked between the gathering storm clouds to shine through the large window in the ceiling. She'd never seen anything like it and it was the main reason she'd selected the little house to rent.

She punched her flat pillow into shape. Maybe she should pull the shades as the light would interrupt her sleep. She hugged the pillow, but didn't get up. Somehow, looking at the moon, knowing it was shining on Haaken this very minute, made her feel closer to him.

It had been just over four cycles and she'd not seen him since she'd left the keep. She'd heard stories as he was the Overseer of Wryven, but she'd not caught a single glimpse. She'd visited the site of the fire and the subsequent reconstruction and she'd seen Ty several times. It had been almost impossible to not approach and ask for news of his brother.

She frowned and turned again, wrestling her pillow into a more accommodating shape. He'd not come for her though he'd sent Mik to act as her watchdog. Across the road from her small cozy home had been a tumbled down shack. Within days of her moving in, Mik and a revolving set of guards had set up housekeeping across the lane. Even now she knew one of them would be sitting in the doorway, keeping an eye on her and her house.

He cared for her. Even if he didn't say it, Haaken did feel something. Why else would he send the guards?

She sighed. Was she wrong to try and force him to say the words? To admit that he loved her and needed her in his life? Even now, she had no answer to the question that burned day in and day out.

She'd proven she could make decisions and take care of herself, and she found she rather liked it. Using her small hoard of gold, she'd single-handedly procured shelter in a small inn upon leaving the castle. After several days of searching, she'd found this tiny, neglected mud-brick house on the edge of the village. After locating the owner, she'd made arrangements to rent the dwelling for a mere pittance.

It had taken days to make the place habitable, as it had been empty for many cycles. But the house was structurally sound as she'd discovered when the first rainstorm had raced through the area. She'd whitewashed it inside and out and scrubbed the floors until they were clean enough to eat from. After purchasing a bed and silk threads, she'd begun her small sewing enterprise by donating an intricately designed altar cloth to the village church. And after the patrons had admired her work, they'd engaged her to sew other pieces—clothing, tablecloths and handkerchiefs. Within a few months, though her gold supply had dwindled, she'd managed to earn enough to pay for her needs. The only item she'd kept was the golden anklet. The gift from him.

Haaken.

Her heart gave a queer little jerk and she closed her eyes. How she missed him. In the beginning, she'd fought to not return to the keep and the security of his embrace. When she was bone-tired and not sure where her next meal would come from, it would have been easier to return.

But she hadn't. She'd stuck to her principles and followed her mind over her heart and she'd succeeded.

You're alone with your principles...

Better to be alone and whole than together and sacrificing everything that was truly important.

Outside the wind cried its loneliness and rain pattered against the overhead window. The freezing season was fast approaching. The trees had turned and soon would shed their burden of leaves.

Dani pulled her covers tighter under her chin as the wind howled through the cracks in the door. Her next project, she thought drowsily, was to replace the door. It was old and needed more than a simple repair. Warped, it didn't fit the frame properly. Only a new one would suffice.

A loud crash and a rush of cold air jarred her from her drowsy contemplation. Muttering under her breath, she heard the distinctive thuds of the door flapping in the breeze.

She reached for her wrap and left the warm cocoon of her bed. Moonlight spilled through the empty frame and a quick glance told her she'd never be able to secure the door again. The thin wood had split around the handle. She'd have to prop it shut with a chair if she hoped to get any sleep tonight.

She hurried over and pushed it shut against the wind. Groping for the chair, she encountered a handful of cloth. Frowning, she turned to see a shadow loom over her.

"Hello, girl."

The scent of cheap ale, tobacco and an unwashed body assailed her and she knew in a minute who it was.

Knot.

She screeched as he slammed his body into hers, pinning her against the rickety door. The foul stench of his body and clothing filled her mouth and nose as his hands pawed her breasts.

"Did you miss old Knot?" His breath was hot and fetid against her neck and she pushed against him, trying to gain distance and breathing room. Where was Mik or one of the other warriors?

She struggled in Knot's bruising grip. He laced a thick arm around her waist and pulled her away from the door. Grabbing a chair, he shoved it under the broken lock to hold the door in place. She gasped as he swung her around and her hip glanced sharply off the corner of the table.

"Now, girl. You're going to give me what you gave *Himself* so freely." He sneered.

Dani swallowed bile as Knot reached between her legs and roughly groped.

She had to keep him talking. Maybe Mik had to answer a call of nature. Surely he'd notice the damaged door and come over to check. Any minute now help would come—

"How did you find me?" she gasped.

"It weren't hard. I remembered the insignia on the horse's bridle." He picked her up and set her on the edge of her table, giving her buttock a hard squeeze before releasing her. "The sire of Wryven is as well known as his shield."

Dani shuddered and tried to push him away, but he pressed closer, his fingers digging into her thighs through the linen of her sleepwear.

"Pretty smart of me, eh?" He gave a short, triumphant laugh. "I wanted you from the first time I seen you." His breathing deepened and one big paw landed on her breast. "And now, you're mine."

The front of her gown ripped and Dani grabbed for the damaged material.

"Knot." She forced a laugh that sounded more like a squeak. "A woman needs time to prepare for a lover—"

"No time."

He grabbed her wrist and shoved her hand out of the way. Dani swung at his head with her other hand, connecting with his cheek.

"Bitch," he snarled. He backhanded her, splitting her lip, and Dani tasted blood. "Fight me, I'll enjoy it more," he hissed.

He slammed her onto the table and stars exploded before her eyes as she heard a roaring in her ears.

I can't lose consciousness...

Her arms felt heavy as she pushed at him. But he grabbed her hips and hauled her to the edge of the table. Spreading her legs, he thrust his hips and she felt the unmistakable ridge of his desire. She shuddered and bile burned the back of her throat. She tried to close her legs against his invasion. He grabbed her wrists when she tore at his hair, his touch deliberately cruel as he twisted her hand back.

"Ahh..." she gagged.

"That's right, cry for Knot—" He pawed the sensitive area between her thighs and she flinched, trying to evade his touch.

This can't be happening...

He held both of her wrists in one hand, then fumbled with the front of his pants and she felt the scrape of his member against her thigh. Summoning her energy, she arched her back and drew in a deep breath.

"HAAKENNNNNN!"

Her cry stunned Knot and he paused, his grip flexing on her arm. He jerked her upright and gave her a vicious shake. "Shut up! You open your mouth when I shove my cock in it—"

He smashed his mouth over hers, smothering her. She gagged as his tongue invaded her mouth and his hand painfully twisted her breast.

The door exploded inward with a crash. The table shuddered as broken wood struck it. A large shadow yanked Knot away from her and Dani rolled to the side, dropping to the floor. Grabbing her tattered clothing, she crawled under the table and saw her attacker yanked outside into the rain.

She scrambled to the door. A cloaked figure dragged Knot across the ground and into the narrow street by his greasy hair. A bolt of lightning lit the sky. Knot howled as he was released.

"On your feet," the tall figure growled.

Dani's heart leapt. He'd heard her...

"She tempted me, sire." Knot rose to his knees, his hands clasped in a penitent pose. "She told me to come to her bed after midnight—"

"Silence," Haaken thundered. "What I saw told a different story." He gestured to a silent guard near the house across the street. "Take him to the gaol. He'll be tried, though I'll be hard pressed to find a jury of his peers. My lands don't harbor scum such as him."

The guard took custody of Knot, hauling him to his feet. Haaken turned toward Dani's house, his stride determined.

"You bastard—"

Knot roared and threw himself after Haaken, his hand raised with patchy moonlight glinting off a slim blade. Dani scrambled to her feet and ran in an effort to intercept them. Haaken must have sensed something was wrong and he turned in a flurry of black leather, withdrew his sword and impaled the other man. Dani skidded to a halt, her gaze on the almost comical expression on Knot's face as he fell to his knees.

Knot looked at the sword buried in his belly, then up at Haaken, sheer disbelief on his face. Haaken withdrew his sword and the man slid to the ground.

Dani swallowed hard as Knot fell face first into the mud. His body twitched twice, then stilled. Her knees buckled and she sank onto the narrow path leading to her front door. Closing her eyes, she lifted her face to the stormy sky, letting the cool rain wash away her tears.

Chapter Twelve

She huddled in the middle of her bed under a pile of blankets. A multitude of candles cast light into every corner of her home. Overhead the storm raged, and she stared blindly at the rain washing over her sky window.

Hushed male voices from the other room told her that the efficient castle guard still worked to remove all the evidence of Knot's untimely arrival. The rhythmic thump of a hammer told her that someone was attempting to fix her broken front door.

She was tired and her body ached where she'd been manhandled. She didn't want to remember his filthy hands on her flesh. Weary, she rubbed her forehead before tucking her hand back under the safety of the blankets. Would she ever be able to forget the nightmare of tonight? It could have been so much worse. Knot could have succeeded in raping her if Haaken hadn't arrived in time to—

"Are you warm enough?"

His smooth voice interrupted her thought. She nodded and tugged up the blanket until it covered her chin. She stared from under the fringe of her hair, her eyes drinking in his massive physique. His dark hair was longer and his shoulders seemed impossibly broad in a gray silk shirt. He'd removed his cape and sword to reveal black leather pants that made his legs look a mile long.

"Why are you here?" Her voice was husky and her throat hurt. If she had the energy later, she'd brew tea before going to sleep. But seeing as she had no energy nor would she be sleeping anytime soon, it was a moot point.

Haaken grabbed a chair from the corner of the small room and brought it closer to the bed. Turning it, he straddled the chair and laid his arms across the back, then propped his chin on his arms. His dark gaze seemed to burrow through the blankets and her skin, into her very heart. "I need to speak to you."

Need, not want. A slip of the tongue? Outside, the wind cried mournfully and she shivered in response. She looked away as she twisted her fingers in the rough wool of her blankets. "What about?"

"I miss you."

Her heart sank. Haaken still couldn't tell her what she desperately needed to hear. Missing her wasn't enough.

"Is that so?" She untwined her fingers and tightened the blanket around her shoulders in an attempt to control her chills. "Well, you've seen me, now was there anything else you needed?"

"I love you."

She stared. "You don't know what love is, Haaken. Your idea of love is to keep me a prisoner—"

"That will never happen again."

"Darn right it won't happen again." She shivered and rubbed her hands over her arms in an effort to warm them. "I won't return—" Her voice caught.

"Dani—"

"No one will ever have complete power over me again—"

"I was wrong." He placed his hand over hers, stopping her frantic rubbing beneath the blanket. "I was wrong to try and lock you up, but I only wanted you safe. The women in my family have all died so young. I only wanted to protect you. I knew you were the one for me the moment I met you and I'm not talking about the mark on your skin."

She frowned. "What mark?"

"On your lower back. The mark of a raven's foot."

"I don't have a mark—"

"Have you ever seen your naked back? Travelers don't usually have the luxury of full-length mirrors."

Her lower back began to itch and she resisted the urge to rub it. Did she really have a mark on her back as he claimed?

Haaken rose from the chair and pushed it out of the way. He removed his boots and placed them by the fireplace. "You're so brave for one with the odds stacked against you. Knowing your owner was selling you into slavery, you still met my gaze and stuck out your chin, daring me to take you away." He removed his shirt.

"I wasn't about to let you know I was afraid," she spluttered. As his golden chest was revealed, she averted her gaze, but it drifted back of its own accord as longing reared its head. "And he wasn't my owner, he was my father." Surprisingly enough the words didn't bring the sting of shame as she'd long feared they would. Instead, she felt—light.

"Your father?" Haaken spat.

"Yes, my father. He sold my sister into slavery as well." Their gazes met and she saw the rage that burned there. "It doesn't matter now, Haaken. Nothing he's done or will do can ever hurt me again."

The muscles in his jaw flexed and slowly his shoulders relaxed. She had a feeling that this wasn't the end of the conversation, but he was willing to let it go for now, for her.

"I knew you were scared," he said. "But you were so determined to face me as my equal." He unlaced the front of his pants.

"What are you doing?" she squeaked.

"Warming you."

She gasped as he tossed his pants onto the chair and walked toward her, nude. Golden firelight danced along the fine line of his body, accentuating his easy grace and hardened musculature. Her woman's mound clenched and flooded with moisture. "You can't be serious."

"As serious as a priest."

He pulled back the blankets and slid in beside her. As his warm body skimmed along hers, she jumped and scrambled for the edge of the bed. The old frame creaked ominously. "There isn't room," she protested.

"Sure there is. You can sleep on top."

She was in no mood for his teasing. She moved to leave the bed when his big hands gripped her hips and pulled her snug against him, spoon-style. His big body touched her from shoulder to toes and the heat radiating from him was heavenly. As he settled her against him, the bed gave another creak.

"It won't hold the both of us," she hissed.

"T'will. This bed wouldn't dare dump the Overseer of Wryven and his beautiful lady to the floor."

Dani stilled her movements. Did he just call her his lady?

He kissed her shoulder and a shiver whispered down her spine. "Come back to the keep with me. Be my woman and stand by my side."

It was all she could do to not scream yes at the top of her lungs. Holding herself tense, she tried to ignore the subtle stroking of his hand on her hip. "Will you lock me up?"

"No, but you must have a guard when you leave the castle. I must know you're safe." His hand moved, brushing the soft curve of her breast. "I have many enemies and I'll not leave you vulnerable."

She shuddered, not because she was cold. She'd missed him so much and it'd been so long since he'd touched her. "Will you let me make my own decisions even when you think I'll fail?"

He chuckled and wrapped his arms around her, one hand claiming her breast and the other stroking her belly. Against her back, his erection pressed into her. "As long as no one's life is at stake, yes, I'll allow you to make your own mistakes."

She twisted in his arms, bumping her nose on his chin. "Promise?"

His solemn, dark eyes locked with hers. "I've never been more serious in my life." He cleared his throat. "I thought I was going to lose you before I could get to you." His voice was tight.

She cuddled into his chest, his heartbeat loud and strong in her ear. "I was so scared."

His arms tightened, but he didn't say anything.

"He didn't hurt me—" He grunted in disagreement and she pressed her fingers against his lips. "He scared me a-a-and tore my clothes—" She shuddered and he kissed her fingers.

"It's over." His voice was rough.

Her nod was jerky. "And you saved me." She gave a short laugh. "My jaJin came to the rescue."

Haaken gave a startled chuckle and hugged her tighter. "I'll put those jaJins to shame—" He cupped her hips and she flinched when he touched the spot where her hip had caught the table. "Are you hurt?"

"I hit the table—"

He sat up and tugged off the blankets. A rush of modesty had her grabbing them for cover, but he pushed her facedown into the bed and ran his hands along her back. She sucked in a noisy breath when he stroked her hip and his touch immediately gentled.

She felt the brush of his lips over her skin and her hands fisted in the pillows as he set about a leisurely exploration of the back of her body. His long fingers kneaded tight muscles as he continued his slow journey. Strong hands stroked the backs of her thighs and, when he found a sensitive area, he stopped and pressed his lips against her skin, acknowledging her hurt before moving on. She giggled when he reached the sensitive backs of her knees. He teased her flesh with the brush of his soft hair before massaging her calves and moving to her feet.

By the time he'd finished with her back, she was warm and limp. She made no protest as he turned her in the narrow bed. There was barely any room for her to move with Haaken filling more than his share of the space, but they managed. Then he stretched over her and nestled himself between her thighs, his cock pressing insistently against her entrance.

He kissed her chin, avoiding her split lip before working his way down her body. Caressing her collarbone, he paused for a nibble here, a gentle nip there. His big hand cupped her breast, his brow furrowing when he saw the faint marks on her pale skin.

Dani said nothing as she laced her fingers through his hair, gently guiding him to her breast. He licked her erect nipple before taking it into his mouth and suckling gently. She made a restless sound and her grip on his head tightened as he laved attention on one breast before moving to the other.

She closed her eyes and concentrated on the sensations he aroused. His hands, deft on her body, stroked and seduced, each movement slow and measured. She shifted, restless beneath him. She wanted him inside her, now. She hooked her leg over his hip and the blunt head of his cock moved into her.

Haaken grunted in surprise and made to move away, but she wrapped her other leg around him, forcing him deeper. "Stay. Please."

He hesitated and she saw his desire mixed with something else. Concern? Love? She didn't know what but wanted to explore it. She arched her hips and he rocked against her, lengthening each motion, and keeping his movements languid, sensual. Each breath that escaped her became a sigh as their fingers twined.

She was in no hurry and she sensed he wasn't either. Buried deep inside her, flesh against flesh, they explored each other's hearts and minds to become one.

The room was warm and Haaken was drowsy. Asleep, Dani was soft and warm against his side and he stroked the baby-soft skin of her back.

He couldn't begin to tell her of the fear he'd felt when he'd heard her scream. He'd just discovered Mik, unconscious with a large bump on the side of his head, when she'd cried out. Haaken had rushed into her house to find Knot's filthy hands on his woman. That act alone had sealed the man's fate and he was heartily glad Knot had died by his sword.

Now, he had her back in his arms and all was as it should be. For the most part at least. All too soon, he'd have to leave her and transform to his animal form for as long as the sun hung in the sky.

He gazed at her sleeping face. Could she knowingly want to spend her life with a half-man/half-beast? Could he tell her he was doomed to animal form forever within the next six months? Was it fair to her to take her heart knowing he could never be the man she needed him to be? Could he ever tell her the truth of the curse?

You must tell her...

But not now, he didn't have to tell her now. Haaken drew the blankets around them and closed his eyes. He still had a few hours before he had to leave.

Chapter Thirteen

Brilliant light roused him from the depths of sleep. Haaken groaned as he rolled over, raising his hand to deflect the intrusion. Where was he? He blinked several times, then lowered his arm.

Above, brilliant sunshine poured through the windows cut into the ceiling. Silent, he gaped at the sight of rich yellow rays shafting into the room and warming the air. When was the last time he'd seen sunlight as a man, not a bird?

He started to sit, then realized there was a weight anchoring him to the bed. He looked down to see Dani, still sound asleep.

The sunlight gave her skin a golden glow and he smiled at the faint line of freckles across the bridge of her nose. He'd never known she had freckles. He'd never seen them before. He tugged away the blankets from her nude body, inspecting her from head to toe in the unrelenting light.

"What are you doing?" she mumbled.

"Looking. Just looking."

She gave a sleepy laugh. "You *looked* enough last night."

But he couldn't prevent the stupidly happy smile on his face. "I don't think I'll ever tire of looking at you."

"Even when I'm old and gray?"

"Even then."

She giggled, and he marveled at the strands of white and gold in her pale hair. "You do say the nicest things." She yawned. "We should get up. We have a lot to do today."

"Are we moving you?" He nuzzled the pearly flesh of her shoulder.

"Uh huh."

"Do we have time for a little side activity before getting to work?" He teased her breast into awareness, her nipple hardening against his lips.

"Mmm..." Her fingers tangled in his hair.

"Your jaJin has something for you." He gave her a noisy kiss on the inside of her breast.

"How *big* is it?" She reached for him, her fingers encircling and stroking just the way he liked. "Not quite huge, but you're getting there."

"It's monumental." He pulled her hand away from his straining cock and placed it over his heart.

She gave him a watery smile as her eyes filled with tears. He kissed her, his touch gentle, keeping her hurt lip in mind. Her mouth trembled beneath his mouth.

"Now I have something for you," she whispered.

"You do?"

She nodded and slid out from under him. Haaken rolled onto his back and laced his hands beneath his head. In the warm light, his woman stood by the bed, a secretive little smile on her face. A rush of anticipation moved through him and his cock responded.

"I think it's time to make myself *your* jaJin." She slithered onto the bed and positioned herself between his legs. Her expression was subservient, but he didn't miss the glint in her eyes. "What do you require of me, master?"

His cock leapt to attention and Haaken chuckled. "I think you know your answer, my beautiful jaJin. I want you to fuck me with your mouth."

Her smile was wicked as she went down on him. Her mouth was hot and wet, and Haaken closed his eyes and gave up to her ministrations, his heart full.

About the Author

To learn more about J.C. Wilder, please visit www.jcwilder.com. Send an email to J.C. at mailto:wilder@jcwilder.com or join her Yahoo! group to join in the fun with other readers as well as J.C.! http://groups.yahoo.com/group/TheWilderSide/.

Look for these titles by J. C. Wilder

Now Available:

Thief of Hearts

In The Gloaming

Deep Waters

Stone Heart

Winter's Daughter

Deep Waters

Adriana by Rosemary Laurey

A lifelong vow of revenge, magic and a love that transcends both.

Adriana has dedicated herself to the destruction of the invading Astrians who murdered her family and destroyed her village. But when she meets an honorable Astrian, she is torn between her lust for revenge and the unexpected love for her avowed enemy.

Warning, this title contains explicit sex.

Nova by J.C. Wilder

In the sequel to *Heart of a Raven (Sacrifice)*, Nova is on the verge of seeing her life's ambition come true when she wins a Merman in a card game. Now she's on the run with her unwanted companion, and with her future in the balance, she finds that the pursuit of her goals could cost this man his life.

Warning, this title contains explicit sex.

Stone Heart

The Shattered Stone by Rosemary Laurey

Tragedy, violence and treachery and a chance encounter that leads to love and the resolution of an ancient dispute.

After her parents die of the Gray Plague, Alys flees the only home she's ever known. She sets off to find her mother's kin in the far Western Lands. On the way she meets the Monarch's envoy, Ranald ven Strad. The chance meeting leads to danger and an astounding discovery.

Warning, this title contains the following: explicit sex.

After the Rain by J.C. Wilder

Li leaves her village after her family's betrayal and seeks to create a new life for herself. She accepts a job at Graystone House as the keeper of the Evil Ones—hundreds of stone gargoyles that fill a chamber from top to bottom and rumored to be the victims of the infamous Lady of Maragorn.

Li only knows that the job fills her with dread, especially when she has to deal with one statue in particular, that of Nikolaz of Riverhaven.

Warning, this title contains the following: explicit sex.

Honor among thieves...

The Gloaming: Thief of Hearts
© 2007 J.C. Wilder

Harper McRae was a woman on a mission. When she'd retired from the life of a professional thief, she never dreamed it would be a family member who forced her back into it. With her stepbrother's reputation on the line, she accepts the task to steal blackmail material a local mobster was using against him. In the midst of one of the most important jobs of her career, she runs into a shadowy figure from her past, Chance, the man who'd broken her heart.

Can two thieves trust each other long enough to escape with their lives?

Warning: Explicit, hanging from the chandeliers style sex.

Available now in ebook from Samhain Publishing.

Country Pleasures
© *2006 Rosemary Laurey*

Journalist Jenny Lee is all set for the chance of a lifetime-an interview in the United Kingdom with a rock star that will boost her career. But car trouble, delays, and meeting a sexy Brit farmer named Rob Castle have her rethinking her priorities.

This book has been previously published.

Warning: this title contains lots of steamy, hot sex!

Available now in ebook from Samhain Publishing.

hot stuff

Discover Samhain!

THE HOTTEST NEW PUBLISHER ON THE PLANET

Romance, fantasy, mystery, thriller, mainstream and
more—Samhain has more selection, hotter authors, and
everything's available in both ebook and print.

Pick your favorite, sit back, and enjoy the ride!
Hot stuff indeed.

SAMHAIN
publishing ltd

WWW.SAMHAINPUBLISHING.COM

GREAT cheap fun

Discover eBooks!

THE FASTEST WAY TO GET THE HOTTEST NAMES

Get your favorite authors on your favorite reader, long before they're out in print! Ebooks from Samhain go wherever you go, and work with whatever you carry—Palm, PDF, Mobi, and more.

Samhain
publishing
Ltd

Printed in the United Kingdom
by Lightning Source UK Ltd.
132591UK00001B/218/P